pornocalypse

M. Satai

Afterhuman Press
2007

ISBN: 978-0-6151-7510-2

"There is, on both sides, something cruel—and even monstrous—in the struggle against an elusive adversary, where the distinguished is opposed to something which cannot be distinguished from it, and which continues to embrace that which is divorced from it."

--Gilles Deleuze

On a freezing cold morning, after a night of debaucheries, you see a
naked girl, maybe 20, 21, chained to a light post along a pathway in
Washington Square Park. She's been raped repeatedly during the long
dark hours, stoned, beaten, burned, etc. Someone who once owned
her, or some nomadic police authority, captured her, used her, and
chained her in the park to die. She's in terrible shape at this point,
blue, bruised, charred, trembling uncontrollably, maybe only a few
hours away from death. She begs, almost incoherently, and through
chattering teeth, for help in a language that's probably Anglo-Sino
gobbledygook. These are her *death labors*. Not only is it unlawful to
help her, but you have no desire to do so. Besides, such sights aren't
unusual. There are others like her all over the city, dead or dying,
offered up for the amusement or usage of passersby. They are
sacrifices to necropolis--a kind of food for the city. You watch her for a
while, her long pale legs, her quivering blue tits, her broken bare feet
plunged in the slushy snow…and you sip your hot coffee and idly
finger your half-hard cock through your pocket with your free hand.
You think about other things: work, food, television. Maybe, before
you move on, you flop your dick out from your fly and piss on the

poor girl's frozen toes. ::That's all the human warmth I can spare,
sweetheart:: Walking against the crowd in Times Square, you get the
sense that you could put two bullets into each of them, one in each
head and one in each heart, and they'd still keep coming forward with
an unsatisfiable appetite for your intestines. It's 4.59pm and I'm on
the 5pm bus waiting for it to depart the station of this city of the
dead. All around me, people are reading their newspapers, brainless.
Outside the window now, a police cruiser parked on a concrete
island. The policeman that was once inside has been assassinated: his
decapitated body is sitting against the grimy brick wall of a soup
kitchen, stripped and disemboweled. I don't consider any of this a
nightmare: what I consider a nightmare is not being able to describe
in all its amoebic immensity that which puts the terror on my face.
We are passing a large, clean, well-kept building: the Senator Frank
Lautenberg Railway Station, which I can easily imagine is a complete
fabrication. Instead, the building is where the bodies are placed in
cold storage—the naked bodies of thousands of attractive young
commuters kidnapped and executed in transit. Project A: it's possible,
of course, that we're all being drained of life-force by the government
as tribute to some alien race. You can consider it a life-tax, and
everyone must pay. It's 5.21 p.m. and I'm sleeping: that means, the
government has come to collect its toll. As I sleep, the life is drained
out of me. When I wake, I feel refreshed and light and filled with
positive energy. It's the feeling one has, paradoxically, when one is
relieved of life. While "asleep," I've been re-programmed to enjoy
dying when I wake up again. That's what it means to *hope*.
(I write this hours after I saw it: a helicopter hanging in the air
overlooking the turnpike as if guarding not us, but *against us*. Was it
something that I was *supposed* to forget: something that I remembered
just now by mistake, in spite of the conditioning?) He sits, upright, in
a wooden chair. Dead-faced, he's typing on a keyboard in a rented
room. Who?

To erect a corpse in the place of any author, *a writing corpse*, that is the
goal, if a goal can be articulated, before the rotten mouth opens and a

terrible all-consuming airborne plague is communicated. *He's a carrier, you see, doesn't suffer from the disease himself. He's immune.* I eat a simulated chicken patty sandwich for dinner: the chicken patty is old, the roll is old. Now, its hours later, and I'm sitting at a small desk in front of a wall of whitewashed bricks as I type these words. It's 9.05 p.m. Tonight it's warmer than its been in weeks: 41F. I've changed my socks and underwear for the first time in three days. On the train, 8.12 a.m., February 10…riding through the deadvilles, the netherwoods of the outlying areas. This is the future: empty streets, empty houses, empty backyards, empty factories. The populations marched away. Outside the necropolis, the suburbs have been reduced to deserts, crawling canker sores. These blighted areas have been re-inhabited by the scattered survivors of pornacalypse who've yet to be rounded up. Once in a while you see one, standing dazed by an old swing set, naked from the waist down. They watch with blank faces the dead trains passing into and out of the necrocity.

Arriving in Penn Station, New York, at about 9 a.m., I see a group of young girls, six or seven of them, poptart-types, huddled together against a tiled wall in a quiet area just off the main concourse. A rent-a-guard in a filthy, homemade uniform waves the muzzle of some kind of large black unmistakably automatic weapon at them. ::Watcha got'em for?:: a businessman in an anti-plague mask asks. The guard grins, toothpick clamped between tight, stained teeth. He indicates the pile of confiscated boots, Nike's, Doc Martens, Avias. ::Criminal footwear. No toes exposed. Not a sandal among them:: The dead-faced businessman laughs, takes a bite from a sloppy breakfast sandwich. Infertile eggs. Pig. Winks. Makes bang-bang gestures with stubby fingers. The doomed girls, barefoot, keen loudly in despair, hugging each other in their bulky parkas and funky fake furs. At their stripped feet lie their piled belongings: backpacks, pocketbooks, department store bags, athletic bags full of haircare products, diet bars, and contraceptive creams. ::We didn't know:: one girl pipes. Blonde-hair pulled back in a perfect ponytail. Small-town cheerleader type. ::We're from Pennsylvania. We just got in. It's

snowing there:: Turning from the guard, she looks in mute appeal at
the businessman. But he's worst than the guard: the dead face
expressionless in white paint. The only sign that anything inhabits
that portrait of total apathy he calls his face is the glint of sadism like
a wire cutter in the black holes of his eyes. The girl's lip trembles. ::
Please:: she says in her daddy-please voice. ::Don't hurt us.:: The
businessman checks his watch: breakfast meeting with Price-
Waterhouse at 10.30 a.m. Must get moving, regretfully. Sobbing,
whimpering, moaning, they hide their faces against each other's
shoulders like bird's against a bitter wind from no-place as the guard
raises the weapon to his hip. *Clackety-clack-clack-click-clackety-clack-clack-
clack.*

Sitting in an office chair, feet up on a bookshelf, I look out the
window: it's 10.44 p.m. Maybe, I think, I'll do some push-ups. So I
do: I do fifteen push-ups. It's easy. I could have done quite a bit
more. What I really need to do is more aerobic exercise. Walking up
the stairs out of the subway this morning, I was winded, calves
cramping. If I had to run, from the zombies, for instance, I'd have
had a fucking heart-attack before I cleared three blocks. This is how
our lives are lived: second by second, heartbeat by heartbeat,
squirting out the hormones, breathing in, breathing out, and at the
end of the day another pile of papers have been written on or
another cinderblock has been stacked on top of the cinderblock
beneath it. In the elevator banks, big men in green jumpsuits talk
loudly and self-importantly into walkie-talkies. They are the only
physically fit ones on the premises. The rest of us, the office cattle,
grow weaker and weaker from the neck down. We pass like ghosts,
or white acolytes, genderless, tending some arcane god through the
artificially over-illuminated hallways. Irradiated. Opening a dictionary
at random, my finger presses on the word: *fare-thee-well.* Who knew
that counted as a *word?* I'm bored—and yet I'm too tired to actually
do anything but write this sentence. I guess I'll try more push-ups.
No, as it turns out, I won't. I pick my nose. Amazing how, when
you're bored, you end up doing something like picking your nose,

when no desire to pick your nose existed immediately beforehand.
With nothing else to do, you suddenly realize how much gunk and
crust is inside your nostrils, how uncomfortable it is just to breathe.
Look at Glamorella, outlaw socialite, strapped into the glory-chair:
the tiara of wires on her pretty head, nipple caps on her pretty
breasts, stimulators on her aristocratic fingers and toes, needle-probes
inserted under the delicate skin of her flawless thighs, wrists, insteps,
throat, etc etc. She's ready for another session, in-between scenes.
Elrod, the hacker bastard, likes to set the digi-volume to just below
2.8 and watch while Glamorella, minus all her Vogue and Gucci and
Park Avenue accoutrements, goes through her *passion* over and over
again, erotically crucified on the Golgotha of every State-induced
sex/rape fantasy she's ever had, broadcast to every television and
movie-screen in the empire translated in the guise of crime thrillers.
It's bad news for the poor girl, shaking and smoking and pissing
herself after only forty-five minutes, that Elrod, wouldn't you know
it, he's written a particularly nasty piece of malware enabling him to
program into her ordeal a few of his own twisted fantasies of
blowtorch love. That'll have them scratching their heads and going
"Huh?" back at the studio. He keeps it going for hours and hours:
Elrod likes to keep it going, he says, until he sees their toenails
shatter. I'm on a train at 5.57 p.m. and waiting for it to leave the
station out of Newark. The car I'm in slowly and unfortunately fills
up with commuters. Is it really necessary, one asks oneself repeatedly,
that there be so many completely unnecessary people in the world?
It's Wednesday, February 11. I'm sitting in front of the whitewashed
brick wall again. Its 7.41 a.m. Last night I fucked her sitting up on the
bed, holding her hips, using her like a fuckdoll. She was dancing in a
strip club, brain zeroed out on drugs, her body pierced and tattooed.
On the stage, she writhed in an oiled-up, masturbatory version of a
burning at the stake. Tiny silver g-string, nipple rings, she was taking
going-nowhere steps on big Lucite platform heels in the hot
lights…Sleep, sleep, and a dream of ants, two ants and an ogre with
an axe…

I wake up, slightly nauseous, dress, have a small cup of espresso. I sit down here. In front of the whitewashed brick wall. Who?

The writer, gaunt and haunted, sits in a straight-backed wooden chair as if awaiting interrogation in front of a desk too small for anything else but a keyboard and a high-intensity desk lamp. Only the desk surface and what lies in its immediate halo is illuminated. The rest of the room is in total annihilatory blackness. If you so much as stick your foot outside this little charmed circle, it may very well cease to exist. The writer sits and stares at the keyboard, at the cursor blinking, on-off, on-off, on-off. His hands above the keys don't move, the fingers frozen in caution. He doesn't want to incriminate himself. The interrogator somewhere in the darkness, *We have ways down here of making you talk*…Everyone talks in the end. Tapes of pigs squealing. Chickens in processing plants. Jews. The writer, bent over the keyboard, fingers hammering away his latest confession: a story about the invasion of a small Missouri town by intergalactic necro vampires who need the chemical energy released by decomposing human flesh to stimulate their own imperialistic reproductive drive. It's a sunlit window with a thin white curtain hanging over it: outside, among the bare trees and slushy dead lawns, birds are singing. *Nothing personal.* The writer says it like a mantra. *Nothing personal.* The drill touches a raw nerve. *Nothing personal.*

Even the scream, *especially the scream*, is disembodied.

Last night, coming out of the grocery store, feeling happy and content, I noticed, as if for the first time, how ugly and tired and unhappy everyone else looked. And then I realized with a shock that this is how most people look 97% of the time. And then, somehow both more and less shocking, I realized that's no doubt how I, too, must look 97% of the time. Without the masks we wear for sex, money, social position, etc., human beings, especially after a certain age, are really quite hideous, even frightening, to look at. What you are looking at, primarily, are all those years of frustration, rage, loneliness, disappointment, unfulfilled desire, etc. that build up like toxins in the flesh. You're looking at untouched bodies, bodies without orgasms, unreleased bodies, *unseen bodies*, poisoned bodies, empty bodies. It's a world inhabited by monsters and monstrosities: you get the feeling that these hideous, grey, happiness-starved zombies might fall upon you at any moment if they catch the slightest whiff of your joy; that they'll tear you limb from limb if they see the least opening, if they can get away with it. That's what the night's for, metaphoric and otherwise. You get the feeling that you have to kill them to preserve your own happiness; that, in effect, it's necessary to kill them *to be happy*.

I'm on the bus now, going through the tunnel, and it's raining. I'm dressed for colder weather, and, after racing to make my connection in order to beat the night, I've broken into a rank sweat. I'm sitting alone and its 5.15 p.m. He steps from the car dressed in purple hot pants and lavender platform flipflops, a short, tight tank-top, his body smooth and softened by the surreptitious hormones he's been ingesting for months. His girlfriend has brought him to the clinic to be castrated and now she leads him compliantly by the hand across the parking lot of the office complex. The "doctor" is an older lesbian who believes in the Cause. These kind of politically-correct gender fascists would rather be slaughtered en masse than listen to reason. ::He'll be so much easier to control this way:: She has the girlfriend lead him to the table, where the feminized boy is quickly strapped into the harness. It's all routine. The doctor casually squeezes the atrophied balls with a gloved hand and barks out a laugh. ::Well, neither of you will be missing these mushy peaches all that much:: Writing is a kind of castration—a feminization process that leads to receptive impotence. One feels as if one might destroy the world by writing, either erase it or appropriate it—both really— one word at a time. It's 5.41 p.m. I'm supposed to be home by 6.30

but it's still raining, and traffic is crawling, and I have forgotten where my home is. Thousands of hungry dead souls, the pornocalyptic diaspora—all going nowhere just like me—fugitives, nomads, refugees, soul-gypsies, but not all of them, not even most of them like me, *I'm writing.*

Rain, rain, rain…the bus is almost two hours late, the bus home. Home, but where? I don't even want to look at my watch. There is no longer any agreement regarding time. I say, 6.30 p.m. but what do I mean? Trees stand in water-filled depressions. Rain. Tailights.

Somehow this seems important: I just took a shit a few minutes ago—a huge, hairy-looking thing, like the root of something dug from the earth, which instantly turned the toilet water the color of whiskey. It was a heavy and thick shit and it smelled, somehow, like a combination of meat and mud. It felt both satisfying and like something of an accomplishment to have delivered myself of this thing: I can still feel its *absence* in the very path it took as it passed through my intestinal tract. Every once in a while, I feel my sphincter contracting on an emptiness…

Monologue: Tarot: Cyclones: Transexuals: Cyborgs: Cancer: Zombies: Slime: Insects: Guns: S-M: Violence, in general: Crows: Nomads.

Imagine me sitting here in a straight-back chair, on a cold February night, letting my hair dry, and having nothing to say. I'm parsimoniously sipping seltzer every once in a while. I'm going to sip some right now. It's difficult to write words as empty and trite as these…and at the same time: it's all too easy. Are you there? I both hope so, and hope not. In the end, of course, it makes no difference. I might as well be semi-conscious, alone in the final moments of my life, having oxygen forced into me with a hose. The bus pulls into the underground station and by now everyone is already dead. A young music student in jeans sits with her blonde head on the shoulder of a slumped businessman. A 30ish woman is bent over a lap full of sales projections with a thin blue drool on her chin. The gas was released into the coach somewhere along the turnpike and death followed relatively quickly. No one suspected a thing: within minutes all the passengers drifted off into a sound sleep. There were some sounds of loud snoring followed by gurglings, soft strangled moans, and death-rattles. But, generally, most died quietly in their sleep and without a fuss. A young Mexican girl has her head against the fogged window, blank brown eyes staring at nothing. Beside her, a bald banker with blue lips and a hard-on looks as if he just dozed off, pen in hand. The temperature has been turned down to just below zero and the men employed in unloading the bus wear biohazard suits and oxygen masks. Most of the "passengers" have defecated into their underwear and the stench can be overpowering. There is also the issue of residual gas still lingering in the coach even after the ventilation system has been re-opened, reverse pumped, and the poison stored in canisters to be dispersed into the generally polluted atmosphere along the empty interstates heading towards the outlawed western lands. A 20-something paralegal is lifted out of her seat. She's lost one of her pumps and the crotch of her pantyhose is soaked with urine. The dark-haired young guy who took the seat beside her falls over until his forehead strikes the seat in front of him. The work proceeds quickly and efficiently: the dead are processed in this way every day. It's all routine. Sleepily, I watch from a seat near the back. A woman with frameless glasses is taken off next. Then, another limp blonde— her freshly-washed hair is passively reflecting the shine of the reading lights. There's a *People* magazine in the aisle. It's opened to a fashion photo-shoot of six celebrities in nearly identical white evening gowns. Are they dead or alive? It's difficult at this point to say, the boundary has been so smeared. *All of this seems relatively humane.* That is what I must admit.

We're talking about the ninth of February at this point, a Monday.
I'm in the office. It's a sunny day, but cold, at least this morning it
was cold. I bought a coffee from a Starbucks on Eighth Avenue. I
went to the office, read my email, and drank the coffee. People, in
general, I've decided, don't interest me very much. This is putting it
lightly. I'd prefer not to bother with them at all. If someone says
something I don't agree with, I pretty much just smile politely and
look someplace other than at their face. It's too exhausting to try to
convince anyone of anything…and even if you succeed, which you
almost never do, what's really gained, anyway? Everyone, it seems to
me, is much too small, one-sided, flat, and without dimension. Do I
make myself clear? One day, and this is one of my sincerest wishes, I
hope to be so apathetic to others that it won't even occur to me to
make statements like the preceding. In fact, I barely have any interest
in making them right now. I barely taken any *notice* of others. How, I
often wonder, in perfect seriousness, can others even exist? I can't
read a book or look at an artwork that doesn't follow the vagaries of
my own mind in real-time, right now, simultaneously to what I'm
actually thinking. The internet is the closest thing to the perfect
artwork. When I'm web-surfing I am creating in text and image the
almost-perfect simulacrum of my own moving mind: but the moment
the session is over the "artwork," like all artwork, is dead. Even if I
could record my online sessions, the result would be an irrelevant
artifact. I'm not interested in looking at anyone else's art or reading
anyone else's text. I can't imagine who'd be reading this. I'd be *afraid*
of the person reading this: their emptiness and vampiric hunger. The
"other" is a monster. It's not a question of having said anything
interesting. What's interesting is what someone might say *next*. The
fact is: *no one ever really says anything interesting.* Because no one can say
what's next, what doesn't follow from what they've said before; no
one can relay anything but what's being broadcast from the central
authority. I'd put a photograph here, if I could: maybe it'd be a
photograph of two dead light-bulbs. One ought to write exclusively
about one's (self) as (un)self-consciously as one can. Such a text
might have the effect of a seemingly chance collision of multiple
speeding automobiles on a complicated freeway—a fatal accident that

keeps on growing outward from its increasingly unapproachable
center at which there is certainly not a single survivor. Sometimes I
forget: don't explain anything. But most of all: don't explain
your(self). Trying to explain anything is one of the biggest mistakes
you can make. The other is to listen to anyone else explain anything.
You will always be ignorant of anything you don't already know. No
one "learns" anything. There's nothing to learn. You just recognize
stuff. "Oh yeah," you say to yourself, "I always thought that."

Only a monstrous text can be the verisimilitudinous product of a
monstrosity—a kind of false (auto)biography of no one possessed by
a multiplicity of cracked voices. That's a thought that I think while
walking up Columbus Avenue in the cold sunlight this afternoon—
about forty-five minutes ago. I'm on my way to buy a Jim Thompson
novel. It's crowded in the bookstore and I feel a nauseous dizziness.
I'm floating behind my dark glasses. I slide my credit card across the
checkout counter: the entire exchange takes place without a word, or
with only a very few. Here's a thought that I think while walking
back: When I use the word "I" it means everything (and everyone)
looked at, inner and outer. *I* is an unassailable masturbatory citadel
that self-destructs in a cataclysmic eruption of multiplicities. When I
get back to the office to write the preceding couple of paragraphs,
someone comes by with a "correction" to some piece of work I'd
previously done. I listen, more or less numbly, talking quickly and
softly in response. It's very quickly clear to me that my female
interlocutor doesn't know what she's talking about. She's only trying
to make her *mark*. I had once thought this woman attractive, had
even considered fucking her, raping her, strangling her, but she looks
fat and unpleasant to me now. Her mouth sags a bit at one side, as if
in prelude to the years to come, and her hair is an unstylish wave of
thick brown nothing. As she's talking, I sip water from a plastic
bottle: these sips of water are like sanctuaries. With each sip, I close
my eyes.

When I open my eyes, she's still there, talking. This is how it is to interact with other people. They stand there, making noises, talking to themselves and no one is listening. There is nothing to say. Everything is post-said. I hear three sounds right now: something being chopped on a chopping block, a kid reading the flap of a book cover, and a very faint mechanical whine. But I'm clearly not anywhere it would be possible to hear any one of these sounds. Where am I?

A long day of errands follows all that…in each shop someone is trying to sell me some overpriced trinket or other. Each of the shopkeepers trying to survive the pornocalypse. In one such shop, a horrible looking woman resembling a dog with orange skin tells me how her sister is looking for a boyfriend. ::She looks 10, but she's 40. It's so hard to meet people now-a-days,:: the dog-woman says. I agree with her out of habit. ::Yes, yes, so hard to meet good people these days:: I smirk. This is a bad hair-day for me. That was yesterday. Here she is, dancing in the midst of pornocalypse, the whore I'm dreaming about, me. Now it's today: February twelfth, a Thursday. I wake up to banging nails. In this part of the city, the new Afro-centurions have taken over. On a line of wooden crosses, white men, stripped naked, are hanging, writhing in agony. Not yet planted, a man lies on his back on a wooden cross that's still lying flat on the ground. ……….I was interrupted by yesterday and I didn't finish my report of that crucifixion of a dozen or so whites by one of the ruling Afro-Centurion gangs now scattered throughout the necropolis. Well I don't feel like talking about it right now, but I'll no doubt come back to it later. No doubt. What happened yesterday to interrupt me? Nothing much. Just a day, like almost all days, filled with hours of pointless busy-work, trivialities, minutiae. These are the kind of days they want you to have: the kind of days that cause you to forget about the stroke that's coming, the clogged arteries, the gut-sack full of cancer, the zombies…

I got two blowjobs, one in the morning and one at night: what more can you ask for?

This morning it's February thirteenth. I heard the date on the radio while I was driving south at 6 a.m. through the dark, cold, empty streets. I wonder how they agreed upon that? Already, I thought to myself, we've blown through nearly two months of the new year. Life passing. Now I'm on a bus heading north at 7.08 a.m. North? There's really nothing to say and although that doesn't always stop me from saying something this time it does...................................
....
.... something's missing here, a passage recorded on another machine, now lost, stolen, confiscated by agents of the State. It doesn't make any difference, not really, but I thought I'd indicate it all the same. It's the fourteenth of February, 9.45 a.m., *their* time, at the moment. I'm sitting in my car, looking at some dry pine trees. They are the kind of pine trees that look like the ones that cling to the thin soil on the sides of rocky mountains, or that the Japanese miniaturize for bonsai. There's some leftover snow on the ground. Now I'm looking at a mailbox with a hole punched in it's side. It's nailed to a crooked wooden post with a red balloon tied to it. The zombies are living here now...you can *feel* them. It's like a bomb was dropped here turning the place into an instant "no-man's land." Jim Thompson says: "You can still be polite to people and not give a damn about them." That's good advice, about the best advice you can take from anyone...especially in the office, the mall, the freeway, wherever you see them: people, so-called. Be "polite," the way you'd be with a poisonous snake or a wolf in the night, or even a rabid squirrel...that's a rule of survival. It would be an interesting experiment, I think, to drop from a small private plane, thousands of explicit x-rated fliers onto this quiet suburban neighborhood of the dead—fliers depicting interracial anal sex, lesbian water sports, threesomes, gay ponyboys, and extreme S-M falling quietly on dead lawns, getting caught in the shrubberies, drifting over swing-sets and gas grills, coming to rest on patios and pool surfaces. It's true, I'm

not a proper chronicler, I'm not a paid spokesman, I'm not an accredited source. I'm not on the "approved" reading list: that's because I'm telling the *truth*. What's the truth? *Whatever you don't want to hear.* I'm writing in secret, under aliases, in abandoned basements and bus stations and all-night diners. I'm a nomad of the keyboard hammering out these reports sitting on park benches or in coffee shops or in parked cars or between sitcoms or errands or whenever everyone is asleep or distracted or otherwise paying me no mind. Then I can slip away: when I'm not being *watched*, when I'm not pretending to be convinced, or blind, or whatever they want you to pretend...when I'm not working to make believe I can't *see*. Sometimes I wonder if there aren't others like me, others that can see, others scribbling away in solitude and secrecy—liquid agents, artists of corrosive graffiti, paradigm terrorists. I wonder. All I see are flat-men, walking mirrors, surface soldiers—me, too, that's what I am, after all: a human being.

Sequentiality...what's that? In my "real" life, what's that? It's February sixteenth now, a Monday. What happened to February fifteenth? The sun came up, the sun went down, and in between...a collage of events that add up to a lot of nothing. On the side of the highway, thousands and thousands of white stones marking the internment camps of the dead. Empty now, after the pornacalypse. So many dead—just think of all the dead. How did we think we could ever contain them all? What insanity led us to think they could be exiled, banished forever? When they finally rose up, they swarmed all over everything, overcoming all our defenses and immunities, flooding the malls and office buildings, taking all the tables in Starbucks, looking out from every TV and movie screen. In every x-ray, you could see the dead looking out. Like a cancer cell, they had taken over the whole operation, all the machinery, they had become "it," or we'd become It. You couldn't get rid of one without destroying the other anymore. ::This is a suicide mission senor. No one gets out of here alive:: The freedom fighter faithfully straps the bandolier of explosive plague canisters across his chest. Each canister

filled with holy water. He walks, dead-eyed, into a crowded square of
zombies as if staring into the promised land. The headline in
tomorrow's newspaper reads, Terrorist bomb kills 45. Do you
understand? ::I am a rogue cell. I am the disease and the cure. I am a
murder-suicide:: We make jokes passing the graveyard, or don't look,
or don't mention it at all, as if the blank concrete buildings weren't
what they were. As if the oily black smoke weren't processing. As if
all those monuments meant that what had happened was now only a
memory, history, that it wasn't all still happening right now. We are
the slaves, and among us, the Invisible Ones, culling us for the
furnaces, the underEarth box-ovens, the entire planet a colonized
concentration camp. Do you wonder where injustice and atrocity
come from? We are imitating Life. I don't know. The self as police-
state. I don't know. What do I mean when I say anything that I say?
There is a flurry of words behind which I hide—behind which I
escape: I=It. Camouflage-nihil. Hiding no-thing. The text as a zigzag
flight through zombie-land. *LA HABRA, Calif. (May 9)- An Orange
County man cut off his mother's head with a circular saw and then died after
trying to decapitate himself, authorities said. Police answered a 911 report of a
family dispute at a Pinehurst Avenue home just after 5:30 a.m. Tuesday, entered
a locked bedroom and found the body of 60-year-old Guadalupe Ruiz on a bed,
police spokeswoman Cindy Knapp said. Arthur Ruiz Jr., 32, was on another
bed with the saw nearby. He had died of neck injuries, police said. It was unclear
why Ruiz attacked his mother, police said. A neighbor, Paula Sanchez, said she
heard the saw before going on a daily walk but thought someone was doing work
in the house or yard." If it would have been a gunshot or something, I would have
called the police," she said.*

It's 5.30 a.m., a Wednesday morning, February eighteenth, more or
less. There's a man on the bus off to my left reading the obituaries: all
the lives that have come to a full-stop, all the unfinished stories. On
the parkway, driving through the darkness, almost alone on the long
black road what one realizes, suddenly, is that there is really no
misery or loss that lasts more than a relatively short and finite time.
And if one can overcome the natural full-body inward flinch there are

always ways of escaping the nosedive our lives might take. This is a comfort, of course. It's a comfort to realize we aren't compelled to live, that not only can the whole project be scrapped at any instant, *but that it will inevitably be scrapped.* I walk, naked, over frozen fields towards the zombies. Each and every one of us, living, is covered in meat. Life is suicide. I don't know. In bed that night, after another failed erection, he learns that he'll have to wear heels and capri pants to work the next morning. ::But everyone will know:: he protests weakly:: She playfully tugs on his limp penis. ::But silly, everyone *already* knows:: The next day, in snug white hip-huggers and open-toed slip-on pumps, he clickety-clacks down the hall between the offices, pushing a little mail-trolley. His ass, fattening lately, jiggles beneath the thin material of the pants. He stands at the xerox machine, mindlessly feeding paper into the tray, blushing, as the other girls, secretaries and assistants, giggle and gawk at him.{whisper, whisper…} ::He's getting sorta chubby in the butt:: one says. ::I think he's wearing a bra,:: says another. His new boss, an up-and-comer, has him making lunch appointments with his old contacts, fetching coffee for visitors. During his own lunch-hour, after a hasty meal of cottage cheese and low-cal fruit salad at his deskette in an open cubicle, it's down to the corner for a touch-up on his weekly pedicure. You are aware, perhaps, that this is February 19 nineteenth, a Thursday. It's 5.10 p.m. The sun is setting. Think of the hospitals: of all the diseased meat taken from people on this very day. They lie on beds, stitched up, groaning, with something missing. And all that stuff missing, taken all together, the diseased mass of it, discolored, lumpy, leaking virulent sauces…well, what kind of separate being might such a pile comprise, what kind of provisional assemblage do such organs without a body form? That, I think, would be *zombie.* Imagine a dream—a nightmare, really—without a dreamer: a common office stapler, for instance, that suddenly came alive and began eating its way across the floor. You see a woman's body, nude, by the water-cooler, a row of heavy copper staples stapled across her belly, slanting across the mastectomy crater of her left chest, piercing her cheek, puncturing the skull bald on one side due to trauma…Why are you here at this hour of the night? Where is

security? On the other side of the floor, you can hear the sound of
chattering, of something machinelike and repetitive, that keeps coming,
that seems to know without knowing anything, that can't be fooled
because it cannot think. Death-machine. Zombie.

Cut to: A jewelry store and a woman looking at diamond engagement
rings. Or is that a man, feminized, dressed in skirt and open-toed
pumps, admiring the sparkle on his pretty finger? Beside him, a fat,
balding, middle-aged lawyer-type looks on with evident satisfaction at
the tranny's narcissitic self-absorption. He's practically licking his fat
lips. ::*I have such plans for you my darling little faggot::* Cut to: A sushi
restaurant and a couple eating what are being called "Harvest Salad
Happy Happy" rolls on the menu, but what everyone suspects is
really rolled inside the rice are delicately-sliced strips of human flesh.
How delicious it tastes with wasabi and ginger! Back in the kitchen, a
Japanese woman in a kimono designed for restaurant wear, tends to
four naked bodies: a pair of teenagers, a housewife, and a man of
about forty, all kidnapped randomly. The victims haven't been
shaved and washed yet. The man, lying on his back by the washbasin,
has a long blue hose emerging from the narrow cheeks of his ass,
brownish water dripping from the puckered hole. His pale belly is
horribly distended. Cut to: Two bodies sleeping in an unmade bed, in
a twilit bedroom, under twisted blankets. The bodies are nearly
naked, dark-haired, a man and a woman, ostensibly, but from a
certain perspective of distance, increasingly similar, increasingly
indistinguishable from each other—one might *almost* say: identical.
They are curled into each other like twin fetuses, or albino peanuts,
like kidneys, perhaps, or some kind of white psychic sex glands. Two
bodies dreaming separate dreams. They could be the next victims of a
serial killer, of a killer watching them, reflecting upon them, unseen,
like god, even now. Did I say they were both sleeping? That was a
mistake. *One of them is wide awake and looking right back.* Days pass. It's
Monday, February twenty-third. I'm sitting in the window of a
Starbucks at 6.41 a.m. My leg hurts. Has something gotten inside it? I

have to take a shit. I don't feel like talking about the well-lit white wooden church yesterday. I don't feel like talking about the zombies on the outside…or is it the zombies on the inside? Or is it both? I can't be bothered to make the distinction between the dead and the dead. *When something is thoroughly rotting you can't tell the difference between inside and outside.* The first thing that begins dissolving is the border. In glass chambers above the massive pipe organs, on each side of the altar, a dead girl, naked, in a sheer white wrapping. You can see the flat milk-giving aureoles. The dark triangles. Dead girls all over. Sipping coffee in café's. Talking on cell phones. Driving cars. Jogging by with headphones. Big-eyed dead girls. Blonde dead girls. Pony-tailed dead girls. Bicycle-riding dead girls. High-heel-wearing dead girls. Dog-walking dead girls. Every cunt that walks passed is a mass grave, a mouth full of worms and lies, an infection, an inoculation by way of ripping out a chunk of groin flesh ::*Kiss me, kiss me*,:: the dead bride says. **This is not a marriage—it's an infection.**

....
....
...............................Damn, where was I, what happened? Have I been unconscious? Has another section been stolen, censored, extracted from the record? It's February twenty-fifth now, a Wednesday, so they say. I don't remember a thing. Was I given a shot, was something removed from inside me, was something else *put in?* Have I been temporarily dead? At a café on the Rue Denis, I read this story in the *New York Times:* **Serial-Killer Delivers "Flowers of Evil"** Who would have thought it would be like this, carrying around a valise of dead assholes through the city? When I thought of becoming a serial killer, I thought it would be a lot more glamorous somehow, a lot cooler. I didn't figure that there was a guild system in place. I didn't plan on serving a fucking *apprenticeship.* I wouldn't have thought that whole hierarchical organizational bullshit would have saturated even to this level. I figured this was still a fancy-free kind of profession. Off the books, off the wire. You know, hang loose,

freelance, anything goes. I pictured myself more or less just running amok with my scalpel, my bone-saw, my ice-pick; that there'd be a lot more freedom to it all. Who could have guessed that serial murder nowadays was a lot like buying a fried chicken franchise? Licenses, registrations, certificates of inspection. I should have known, I guess. Nowadays you can't even be a poet without paying a licensing fee. Goddammit, they put the pinch on you at every fucking turn. Krentz lives on West 87th. His place smells of old milk, old hair, old books, old dust, old boxes full of old nothing. That makes sense: Krentz himself is old, seventy, eighty, ninety, so old the fucking number doesn't make a difference. He's got no teeth anymore, no eye-sight, no hard-on...nothing hard. He sits, dressed in a smelly bathrobe, melting away in a soft musty armchair, looking at the glossy pages of bird magazines. What's he listening to today? Rachmaninoff? Dvorjak? He reaches for a glass on the table. His liver-spotted hand trembles. ::Have you come to deliver my precious bouquet, my darling boy? My wrinkled brown rosebuds?:: His voice crackles and croaks. It laughs by rheumatic fits and starts. Bastard, he can barely keep the spit in his mouth. Wet, spastic mouth, like an asshole itself, it is, like a constipated asshole, slick with a freshly administered enema, trying to work out a turd. Drunk, on top of everything else—Christ, how I want to smash his skull to pieces with the nearly empty decanter at his side. I want to see his putrid brains—a colorless fluid by now I'd suspect, lifeless, like sterile semen. Do you know what I have to do, what risks and commotion I have to endure to collect his dozen assholes? And why assholes, of all things, dammit—why must I be subject to *his* inane fetishes when I'm doing all the work? The meeting in bars and health clubs, the wooing, the convincing, the goading, the seducing, the threatening...and then the slaughter itself, the dragging and yanking, the stink, and the mess in the bathroom, coring out a rectum when you're covered in sweat and blood and slipping in the shit all over the place. And the fucker knows, old and drunk and senile as he is...he *knows* if I bring him an asshole that isn't *fresh*, that belongs to some dishwashing hag over fifty or somebody's grandma. You'd have to see it to believe it, watching him poke that ugly hooked beak of his over the wrinkled brown hole of some seventy-year-old shut-in I conked out on the Upper East Side. The repugnance on old Krentz's face, the disapproving look he gives me. And it's no use trying fool him either—its not any use at all washing them assholes all pink and rosy, plucking out the white hairs, and trying to sell him on the idea that it belongs to some thirteen-year-old mallrat, oh no sir—that would make my life too fucking easy. No, that nose of Krentz's, that hideous, obscene, gnarled vulture beak of his can smell a fresh asshole a thousand miles away and a putrid aged one from two ::There are no short-cuts to serial killing boy:: the old fucker slobbers all over me and I feel the neck of that whisky decanter in my sweaty grip, I feel the heft of it thunk fatally and oh-so-satisfyingly on his soft skull as if I'd actually picked it up and hit him with it, as if I had the balls to do it. Instead, I hand him the still slightly bleeding assholes all bundled up in florist tissue paper that's gone damp and pink. He can read my mind, I guess, no, that's not it: he can smell *my* asshole. He can smell the excitement in it, the betrayal, the arousal, the death in it, the something-being-born-in-it. He cackles and hacks. ::I'll fuck you up the ass, son. Yeah, you better watch your asshole, boy. Old Krentz will get ya in the end, he'll get ya where a sittin'. Boo!:: And on and on like that. Senile ramblings. Just old man ranting and raving is all it is. You know how it goes--*you know*. Fucking father-figures, teachers, priests, mentors…the whole rotten lot of them. You have to listen—you have to take it up the ass. At least until you don't have to take it up the ass anymore. *Until you can't take it anymore.* Fucker, he's right after all. Sitting up in that decaying bachelor's apartment, rotting away, flipping through his bird magazines, sipping ancient whiskies, sniffing his bouquet of leaking assholes. That's the future, that's me—and that's only if I'm lucky. *I can't take it anymore.* And then some time passes and I think…………………………………………………..Yes, I can. I can take it. In any event, I do. I take out my pad and jot down a short to-do list: 1. Stop believing in the existence of myself. 2. Stop believing in the existence other people. 3. Stop believing in Him. There are small black checkmarks next to the first two items. How though. What do I have to do to be able to put a check next to number 3? One day I'll core the mouth out of that old shithead's face, that sloppy asshole-mouth of his. I'll carry his brown puckered lips in my bag like a dried-out slug, that'll be the day, the last fucking rose I'll ever pluck and I'll deliver it to myself—well, to no one really—and the gift will be that he'll have finally stopped talking, that I won't hear him anymore. Anyway, I spend the rest of the afternoon sitting in a café', hating everyone around me, and sipping tea while looking through a copy of *The Image*, a pornographic novel by an author named Jean deBerg. It's not too interesting, I think, all the talk about erotic sacrifice and the girl doesn't even die in the end. I keep asking dead author, the non-existent characters, the ink and paper on the table in front of me, *Where's the romance in that? Where?*

And now it's February twenty-sixth, a Thursday, and it's around 8.30 a.m. **Zombie point-zero.** I think of a writer, sitting alone in a room, writing just before dawn, scratch, scratch, like mice in the plaster walls…and, then, something suddenly slips out of his head, leaks out of his ear, maybe, a cold black trickle down the side of his neck. Or it might leap, like a frog with fur and a monkey's face, off the top of his shoulders, and land with a sliding *splat* on the other side of the room and stare up at him with huge, nocturnal eyes, blue lips grinning, with a sharp-toothed, monkey-gibberish grin. No, no…that is how the writer might describe it later, how he might personify it in retrospect, how he might *fictionalize* it. What it would really be…it would be a blob, a formless phlegmy mass, greenish-yellow, like a pus or the nameless leakage from an infected wound, but somehow *alive*. **Zombie-infection.** The writer would be horrified, disgusted, terrified by this *thing* that had come out of him and he'd want to destroy it, to erase it, but, of course, that would be impossible. As sick and afraid and revolted as he might be, he'd also be fascinated at this self-emission, the way one is fascinated by a nose-picking, or a particularly heavy load of shit, inasmuch as it was formed inside, that it issued from the dark cavities of his own body. He'd be fascinated and unable to destroy his own creation. And this viscous wad would *walk*, crawl, really, sidling, crablike, amoeba-like, out of the room, the writer's room, and into the city. It would slip into the water supply, into the subway system, into the rat population, into the ventilation ducts of office buildings, etc. etc. etc., each etc. a glyph for how one thing leads to another thing, leads to all things, *Everything is Everything.* **Zombie-apocalypse.** Organs without a body...the diseased slop, disconnected, sick, gall-bladders, pancreases, lungs, stomachs, miles and miles of intestines, all taken out of context, without the boundaries of flesh, the border of bone, not lifeless, but *all life,* such unmitigated, unspeakable *horror.* To imagine what might be large enough to encompass all these discarded organs, this inassimilable diseased *slop,* you'd have to imagine god It-self, you'd have to imagine a towering zombie-god, you'd have to imagine life as death, an assemblage of way too many parts, an aggregate-machine so complex, short-sightedely, and randomly designed as to be rendered completely useless. A God vomit. *You'd have to imagine a monstrous machine that produces nothing.* Zombie. **Zombie-industrial** Necropolis, now, is filled with the hasty construction of these cancerous machines, spreading, organically and chaotically, across the landscape in a provisional and opportunistic way. And outside of each factory, feeding these immense, nonstop zombie-machines, the people of necropolis line up, patient and docile, like slaughterhouse cows, businessmen, mothers, architectural design students, marketing directors, daycare workers, grammar school teachers with entire classes of nine-year-olds in tow, all that traffic lined up outside the tunnels, stalled on the bridges, coming into the airports...all of them walking *orderly* into the open and irresistible mouth of the zombie. *Hurts so much...I'm so thirsty...hurts...why don't they give me something to drink...god, I'm so cold...what's that sound, that sound, why won't anyone come, why won't anyone, where is everyone...momma...*

"The fortress of obscenity cannot be brought down."

–Jean Baudrillard

Billy hears the men come into the jail. They're drunk, rowdy, cursing. The police chief says ::You know the rules, gentlemen. You got till dawn. You don't kill him, you hear? Don't mark up his face too much neither. Girl's got a big day tomorrow:: ::Har har haw har:: the mob says. ::Har har haw har:: The laughter was harsh and crude and filled with hatred. *Why do they have to be so angry?* Billy wondered. *Even if they want to kill me. Why do they have to hate me?* He sits, trembling, against the cold stone wall on the narrow cot in his cell. The men, jeering and cursing, are coming down the short hallway, opening the clanging iron door with drunken awkwardness. He can recognize their voices: Mr. Harrow, from the drug store; Mr. Jenkins, the school wrestling coach. Mr. Tyler, the fertilizer farmer. Mr. Dawkins, his dad's friend…they were all men that Billy had known all his life, had seen in town, at school, at home. He closed his eyes, shivering, as noted, holding his knees against his chest. He has accepted his fate; there was no use fighting, couldn't they see that? He would go meekly, cooperatively, he wouldn't give them any trouble. Couldn't they see that? Didn't it matter? Why did it have to be like *this*? They had already burst into the cell and someone yanked him off the cot and threw him to the stone floor. He could feel their hostility, the naked lust for violence radiating from their bodies, the warmth and perfume of it, as they looked down at him as if he were some sort of insect cringing in the light. The white spaghetti-strap dress he wore had tangled around his long smooth legs and he'd fallen helplessly with a soft gasp. Someone yanked him back to his knees by his ponytail and smacked him hard across the cheek. Someone growled derisively to the man who'd struck him. ::Remember, what the chief said, don't fuck up kewpie doll's face:: Billy tasted blood in his mouth, felt bearded lips in the shell of his ear. ::I'd kill you right now if worse weren't in store for you, you little faggot:: A chorus of drunken hoots and hollers followed. Billy felt Mr. Dawkins, he was sure it was Mr. Dawkins, pull his head close. The old man's hot sour breath burned against Billy's lips and the drunken man leered ::You don't want that Pepsodent smile busted up girly then I better feel nothing but tongue. Open up queer:: And Billy tasted hot salty flesh inflate in his mouth almost immediately, the sour meat nearly gagging him as his head was clamped fast between two all-powerful hands and he had no choice but to suck, to suck or to suffocate. Within moments, it seemed, the jism blasted against the back of his throat, the slime of life, and Billy gulped it down, gulped it down as fast as he could. A moment later, he felt a cock forced into the tight rubber ring of his rectum and then another, long and cigar-thin, stuffed into his bruised mouth. He was beaten with fists and straps and sticks, dragged out of the cell and into the yard where he was strung up by the wrists with leather thongs to a post in the dust. He was beaten some more there, and raped, repeatedly. Many of the men came back for more. It was as if they inspired each other to greater acts of arousal and cruelty. Even the old men, unable to penetrate him, rubbed their wrinkled genitals in their arthritic hands and leaked their impotent cum on his bruised body. A crowd had gathered by then, and Billy, his once beautiful white dress in shreds and tatters, knelt limp and bleeding in the halogen lights of a circle of parked SUVs, as the men abused him over and over and over. ::Don't break any bones, bitch has got a long walk down the aisle tomorrow:: someone shouted over the drunken mob. More laughter. Shouts. Someone sing-song answers ::She's getting married in the morning:: A fresh howl of laughter. They had taken him down from the post, dragged him across the yard and suspended him from a kind of overhead beam at one point, his bare feet nearly clear off the ground, as he struggled to keep his balance on painted tiptoes, hopelessly struggling to relieve the pain in his wrists, his arms feeling as if they were being pulled clear from their sockets. They took turns. Someone had Billy's narrows hips in their vise-like grip and gave it to him up his now gaping and bleeding asshole with such violence that the rape, even after so many others, penetrated Billy's dimming consciousness. It wasn't until his rapist came into his rectum that Billy realized it was Grant, the thick-headed jock who used to bully him in high-school. At one point, Mr. Taylor, the mechanic, came forward with a leer and a circlet of twisted barbed-wire in his outstretched hands. ::Wouldn't wanna forget your tiara, would ya Barbie doll?:: How they laughed, how the crowd of them howled with a cruel and cosmic humor when the barbed-wire tiara was pressed onto Billy's head. ::How's that princess?:: Mr. Taylor drawled. ::Why she's pretty as a picture in a fairy tale:: someone else shouted. Sometime later, Billy regained consciousness. He was back in the cell, lying curled up on the cold floor. His dress, once so beautiful, had all but dissolved into a puddle of bloody confetti. Around his throbbing head, the tiara of barbed wire seemed to be stapled into his skull. Every part of his body felt bruised and lacerated and no place more than his poor, torn-open asshole. He could feel the cum of other men like a wad of something alien boiling and roiling inside him and he could taste their mixed seed in his mouth, a taste so bitter and dirty he knew it would never wash away. But worse of all, the sun was up. Billy could tell the sun was up, even in the basement of the police station where his cell was located. He could see it the way the light spilled from the heavy door at the end of the hall that had just swung open. The deputies were coming for him. He could hear the sharp footsteps of their polished shoes on the polished floors. He could hear their loud, aggressive, excited voices. They were coming, coming to walk him down the aisle. Billy closed his eyes. *The worst had come.* But no, not yet, there would be a brief respite. The worst was still yet to come. Now it was his sister Kathy and her best friend Jenna who had come to the prison with his wedding dress and heels and to do his nails and hair for his last "date". That seemed fitting, somehow. It was just like the old days, Jenna remarked, as they chatted and fussed with his makeup, referring to the times when the girls would play dress-up with a seven-year-old Billy. They'd style his hair, paint his nails, and

make him wear one of their own outgrown dresses. Then they'd
force him to totter around in mom's high-heels or one of the girls'
sandals. Over his weak protests, they'd show off their new little
"sister" to the rest of the kids in the neighborhood. Everyone
laughed and teased and some of the adults even said how Billy made
just a darling little girl. His father looked askance at cross-dressed
little Billy, that sharp gleam in his eye. It seemed a harmless game at
the time. Now, fifteen years later, they were playing their seemingly
harmless little "game" for the last time. Neither Kathy nor Jenna said
much about what would happen over the next twelve hours. They
kept the conversation light, confined to such concerns as whether to
highlight Billy's hair, what color to paint his toenails, to accessorize
or not to accessorize. To Billy, it all seemed so surreal. ::Will mom
come?:: His sister brushes out Billy's hair while Jenna tries to
convince the guard to let them run an extension cord from the
electric outlet in the guardroom so the girls can operate the mini
blow-dryer. They'll need a basin of water, too. ::Goodness, Billy,
you're so yucky!: The girls have decided to give Billy blonde
highlights, after all. ::Mom's really mad at you Billy. But I'm pretty
sure she'll come to see you before, you know, the day's over. After
all, she did pick the dress and everything. So its not like she doesn't
care.:: It was a beautiful dress, all concurred. The girls took it out of
its protective cocoon of plastic and hung it on one of the cell bars to
cheer Billy up: a long, white sheath cut sexily up the side to show off
his pretty legs. The shoes his mom had picked out were dreamy:
sequined high-heeled sandals in just his size. Billy is philosophical. ::I
guess you're right:: ::You have to understand,:: his sister explains,
::Mom was really disappointed at the way things turned out. You
being a sissy and all. And the way it effected Daddy, well, you've got
to understand that we're *all* very upset with you.:: Billy whispers ::I'm
sorry:: doe-eyes downcast. ::It's not your fault. We all know that deep
down, even Daddy, I'd guess.:: Jenna returns from her flirty
discussion with the guard. ::It's that bitch Becca that did you in. What
a shameless little whore.:: :::She didn't mean it,:: Billy objects softly,
forgiving everyone. ::Oh you silly girl,:: his sister says. ::When are you
going to stop apologizing for that vicious bitch? She did too mean it.

She knew she was betraying you. They made her a deal, for crissakes. She doesn't love you at all you know. She never did. She's been screwing Grant behind your back the whole time you've been together practically. Oh what difference does it make anyway? You should never have come back here, Billy. You should have never come back knowing what you *are*. You should have stayed in Freak City with the rest of the freaks, just like Daddy says. Now let's do your nails. I mean, we don't have a ton of time to fix you up.::

It's March 2nd, no, make that March 3rd: and it's 1.45 p.m. on a Tuesday. The weather has grown warmer, the soil thawing wherever there's soil, and you can almost sense the emergence of bald skulls, like cheap buried pottery, pushing through the sites of last year's gardens. Where is that girl I buried last fall? I lived with her for a while, keeping one eye open even while I slept, but the strain grew too much to bear. I never knew when her appetite might get the better of her. I never knew when I might wake up one morning screaming and bucking with pain, finding her astraddle my waist, and one of her arms up to the elbow in my abdomen, her greedy hand clutching around somewhere in my entrails, searching for...what? The suspense itself was killing me, the suspense of waiting for her to attack: it was too much. It was driving me insane. So I killed her. If she were a disease, it would have been called an inoculation, or if she were a pre-cancerous polyp or cyst, killing her would have been considered a sound preventive measure—a form of prophylactic self-defense. And yet, being as dangerous as either a precancerous cyst or virus, being *more* dangerous than either, being the undead that she was, the zombie, it's called "murder" what I've done and I must hide it under the dirt. That's the zombie "ethics" we're coerced to obey, the doublespeak, the ever-running xerox machine of propaganda, the media reverse-image, the totalitarianism of hypocrisy that makes it impossible to stand up for the "real" among an empire populated, no, let's say *haunted,* by images. *You are under arrest for everything.* We're supposed to harbor what will kill us. We're supposed to pretend that it's something other than it is. What? What is it? Human, that's what.

We're supposed to pretend it's *human*. Oh Christ…This morning, it being rather warm and moist, I took a walk to where they'd crucified another one of those sissies. Poor bastard, nearly four hours it took, inadvertently writhing lasciviously on a cross for our amusement, pissing himself, shuddering, and expiring in slow-motion with strangled gasps…how, in so many regards, I envied her. Often, I wish I could die like that, too. One wishes, it seems, for a death so humiliating it would obliterate at once every last trace of the urge to live at all. Imagine: a bomb exploding fifteen or twenty miles above the city but with the capacity to flash-freeze everyone into a kind of white basalt statue so that the city itself would forever after become a human museum through which aliens from a visiting planet might one day wander, or, better yet, which entire rat populations would inhabit, unchecked. *"…to realize other ways to see, to open our thinking and practices to the nomad nomos that creates wandering distributions of assemblages, distributions whose plurality of centers mix perspectives and points of view and open up power to create new social and political institutions not yet envisioned by our current democratic practices." –Dorothea Olkowski*

Ingredients: Filtered Water, High Fructose Corn Syrup and/or Pure Cane Sugar, Pear and/or Apple Juice from Concentrate, Citric Acid, Natural Flavors, Asorbic Acid (Vitamin C), Gum Arabic, Ester Gum, Taurine, Vitamin E Acetate. –Jones Naturals "Berry White: Strawberry, Cherry & Grapefruit"

The plastic red handle, for instance, of a large pair of scissors.

Turn right onto Bridge St./MA-9E.
Turn left on S Pleasant St.
Turn left onto Selles (?) St.

A woman sits on a kitchen counter, oiling up her shiny oiled skin. She assumes the position of a raw turkey, knees tucked under, butt raised, and waits to be stuffed with a concoction of stewed fruits and warm buttered bread. Trussed up tightly, she compliantly opens her mouth wide for the candied red apple. Her eyes widen in surprise when the cold meat thermometer is inserted into her swollen anus. Stuffed so, she looks mildly pregnant. Preheat the oven to 375. Fictionmania.com. Muki's Kitchen. When they take the prisoner away after the sentence has been pronounced, he walks quietly to his fate as if he were cooperating, as if he agreed on some level with the proceedings and the outcome. The impression one gets while watching is one of supreme reasonableness and the ideal exercise of *justice*. The truth, however, is much different. The prisoner isn't cooperating; he's been coerced by the unanswerable might of "judicial" tyranny. The powers arrayed against the prisoner are so one-sided that resistance would be smothered to insignificance within an instant. What elicits his "cooperation" is the threat of overwhelming brute force: the threat of pain and death. He isn't cooperating at all, he's broken. His world has been annihilated by interrogation and imprisonment. His reality has been legislated out of existence. He is not so much a prisoner, but, inasmuch as he's survived at all, such a man is a martyr. God is a nuclear blast inside the "human being." Colorectal cancer.

Bibottom, Submissive Male *Seeking rough, kinky top males for hot action. I love to try anything you have in mind, whatever it is. I love to wear woman's clothes and be your tramp.* –New York Press personal ad

Nutrition Facts: Serv. Size 8fl oz (240ml) Servings Per Container 2.5 Amount Per Serving Calories 0 % Daily Value *Total Fat 0g   0% Sodium 0mg 0% Total Carb 0g 0% Protein 0g *Percent Daily Values are based on a 2,000 calorie diet. --*Aquafina Non-Carbonated Purified Drinking Water*

Make Me Your Woman *Attractive, masculine JM, 33, oral, ISO G/BiM, to try crossdressing fantasies, (I am masculine but want to feel like a woman). You: 40-75, good kisser, kinky, discreet. Your place.* –New York Press personal ad

"A little worried toward the end, she took it well and we were able to cook her up perfectly!" –Muki's Kitchen

...to think that even my deepest moments of solipsistic introversion are an attempt to elicit a "saving" dialogue with the outside world instead of the circular reductive crusade toward the point of no-return and escape into a peaceful oblivion that it should and must be—that disgusts me, that must stop.

"Wednesday, March 3rd. On this day in 1876, a shower of meat chunks, one to four square inches in size, rained down on Bath County in Kentucky. Though early opinion was that it was no more than some sort of vegetable matter, it was determined that the samples studied were cartilage, lung tissue, and muscle. The final conclusion was that the meat had fallen from buzzards or vultures who vomited their meals while flying overhead." –Worst Case Scenario Calendar

Gate 7: where does the bus go to that leaves from there? Oh wait, I know, I'm on it.

The willing victim who, at the penultimate moment, expresses doubt, second thoughts, and uncontrollable trembling panic at the impending orgasm of an overwhelming violence; the catastrophic sacrifice underway and the dawning realization in the (heretofore) complicit victim's eyes that it is already too late to stop or to change one's mind about participating in the carnage; that moment of

abandonment to terror and humiliation on the face of the one who up to
this point has been *only* a "volunteer," the expression which says *oh
my God I cannot go back it's too late*-- that is the rape-within-consent that
characterizes the "perfect" victim and, therefore, most highly-prized
desire-object of all: the sacrifice. *"The absence of otherness secretes another,
intangible otherness: the absolute otherness of the virus." —Jean Baudrillard*
That face that haunts me in the mirror, who is he? I must kill him:
that's me. Suicide machine: a bottle of xanax, one-hundred-twenty
pills, 1mg each, a flask of whiskey, a plastic bag and elastic band, a
black Hyundai Eleantra with all the windows rolled down, a secluded
mountain overlook on a subzero winter night, starry skies. The rape
of everyone, that is what comes to mind when looking at a hillside
covered as far as the eye can see with white headstones. *"Whatever
pain achieves, it achieves in part through its unshareability, and it ensures this
unshareability through its resistance to language…Prolonged pain does not simply
resist language but actively destroys it, bringing about an immediate reversion to a
state anterior to language, to the sounds and cries a human being makes before
language is learned." —Elaine Scarry* Art is an animal-cry with no answer,
a war-cry with no compromise, a sick-bed moan of isolation and
pain, or an assassin's shout as he squeezes the trigger to assassinate
the beating heart of the populace. Art is not communication—but
just the opposite, it's the despair of any possibility of communication
whatsoever. Art is tragic and futile, like a suicide note: because it's
always misinterpreted. It's the last word we never get because nothing
can be communicated, nothing can be explained, "I don't want to
hear your explanations. *It is always irrelevant what the "other" thinks.*
There are no "others."

People, being mainly morons, need a story. *For weeks, he spoon-feeds me
babyfood and fruit sauces heavily laced with powerful laxatives until I really do
become incontinent, unable to go out anywhere without wearing a diaper, pale,
weak, trembly all over…*She waits, less and less patiently, as he bleeds to
death, naked and on his knees, leaning over into the empty bathtub.
She takes her shoes off—it's easier, she says, to wash her bare feet if
they are splattered by his blood and piss than to wash her stockings

and brand-new black velvet pump sandals. ::Don't you want to see my pretty toes one last time before you die?:: What would happen, let's say, if a naked woman on a bicycle were to pedal as fast as she could through a car-wash of whirring razor-sharp blades? Here's a story: John woke up. He went to work. He came back home. He went to sleep. What a story is, ordinarily, is the act of putting a microscope to the minutiae of the little twists and turns of events that allow John to return—or not to return—home to bed at night. Does he dream? Ah, perhaps, and there's the rub. A story provides a moral, is didactic in nature, it seeks to enforce the conditioning of meaning and order in our lives. It lies. It oppresses. It belongs to the control and order that systemizes and suppresses the chaos and meaninglessness of nomadic consciousness. And in so doing, it depresses even as it oppresses: because our lives do not resemble these stories, nor the characters in these stories. In a car, a small, possibly yellow, convertible, I'm talking to the widow of Georges Bataille. But I don't remember anything she says, if she says anything worth remembering. Its raining. Who I am, as if I were a radio, or antennae, or radar dish is unimportant and uninteresting: what I broadcast, what signals I relay, pick-up, from wherever that is unimportant and uninteresting, too. *"A world purged of the old forms of infection, a world 'ideal' from the clinical point of view, offers a perfect field of operations for the impalpable and implacable pathology which arises from the sterilization itself." –Jean Baudrillard* There is hope, then, hope that there will be no cure, that the cure itself will promote the incubation of more resistant, more virulent diseases. What is it, what apocalyptic disgust with the world, that causes me to dream of one day getting in a car and driving west with no destination, simply heading in the direction of the sunset, and following it until I vanish entirely somewhere *short* of the end of the earth? *"If, the anti-humanists argued, 'we' accept humanism's claim that 'we' are naturally inclined to think, organise, and act in certain ways, it is difficult to believe that human society and behaviour could ever be other than they are now. Humanism was therefore to be opposed if radical change, the thinking of difference, was to become a possibility. The future would begin with the end of man." –Neil Badmington* Well, said Mr. Badmington, and thus the writer becomes something alien, no, he reveals himself as something alien, something hostile, not by choice or morality, but by very nature itself. And so if my hands on this keyboard are cold and scaly, sprouting a fine silver hair, you won't be surprised, nor should you be shocked that they are the hands of a natural born killer. *"Writing is always writing **for** animals, that is not to them, but in their place, doing what animals can't, writing, freeing life from prisons that humans have created and that's what resistance is. That's obviously what artists do." —Gilles Deleuze*

Its morning, 7 a.m. or so, and Dad calls his daughter out to the yard. ::Kimberly, its time. Let's go.:: Out shuffles a blonde girl, fifteen or sixteen, in a thin pink chemise. Dad winks. ::Ready?:: ::Guess so.:: The surly teenager shrugs. In the yard, everything is wet and dewy, grill, swing-set, deck, etc. On the street-side there's a wooden trellis covered with early buds, a climbing rosebush. ::No panties I hope?:: No response. Dad frowns. ::Kimmie?:: The teenager shakes her head, rolling her eyes. Dad leers and checks anyway. The little V plucked clean and smooth her day of birth. My little chicken. He helps her up onto the empty bucket, puts the noose over her head. A small crowd of neighbors have gathered: businessmen anxious to catch the seven-ten, housewives holding closed their terrycloth robes and sipping mugs of hot coffee, a few school-kids with their backpacks. The bucket is kicked out from under her without ceremony and Kimberly feels the terrible crush around her throat. She blacks out for a few moments and she thinks, that's it, wow that was fast, I'm dead, but then she's back all at once with a force that hurts, strangling at the end of the rope, sweating, frothing at the mouth, (how gross), and jerking around, her pink toes twinkling above the flagstones. She releases a hot gush of piss: it steams in the chill of the crisp morning air. It's all over within minutes. ::All done, dear:: Mom, standing on the deck. ::All done.:: The neighbors drift off in pairs, trailing the usual neighborhood gossip and chit-chat. By noon, her once pretty face is a featureless mask, swollen like a blue catcher's mitt. Little kids have dared each other to poke off her nightie with sticks: the flimsy now cloth hangs off her waist. They grow bolder. They whack her

legs, poke the sticks up inside her, throw stones at her dangling body.
Rush hour: trucks on the interstate, transporting serial killers for
distribution throughout the Midwest: sexual murder a multimillion
dollar business enterprise nowadays and rapidly growing, one of the
last booming industries. A year or so has passed. They've erected
orange gates over the walkways in the park. From each crossbeam, a
naked corpse hangs, playing peek-a-boo with a heavy orange curtain
that undulates in the wind. Art, they're calling it. My name is...

Starbucks, 69th Street, two large-boned transvestites sit at a table and
pour over a catalog of pliers and wire-cutters. "To many men life is a
failure; a poison-worm gnaweth at their heart. Then let them see to it
that their dying is all the more a success," says Nietzsche. I want to
call X, even though love doesn't exist, but I don't: to do so, would be
to desire what one cant have, which is a weakness and a waste of
time, even if it is the only way out of hell. "...*if one gave birth to a heart
on a plate, it would say 'love' and twitch like the lopped leg of a frog.' –Djuna
Barnes* It's out there, on the streets, a free-floating malignancy, a kind
of black hole with tentacles, variable in size, from a pinprick to a
manhole cover—all the way up to the size of a typical UFO:
monstrosity. Looking in at me, through the Starbucks window, is a man
I take at first to be the ghost of one of the homeless. There are dark
circles around his accusatory eyes, so that he looks as if he had empty
holes in his head, lines are carved into his sunken cheeks, a mouth
pulled down in disapproval and disavowal; it's a wasted face, a
twisted face, a haunted face like its being pulled away by the wind—
its my face, ten years older, and its grinning, *awfully*. To go to the end
of human compassion is to see monsters. The grey dead lurk on
trains, in office hallways, especially near water fountains and
microwave ovens, and in forlorn commonplaces like the empty cereal
aisles of supermarkets late at night. You can only see the dead when
you are absolutely alone, solitary, isolated, beyond all others, when
you've given up all attempts at understanding or hoping to be
understood. Communication, that old illusion, that oldest god.
Isolation=death=enlightenment=torment=Ecstasy. It's a shamanic

equation. Understanding is a kind of communal blindness: it's a contract agreed upon among the huddled masses *not-to-see*.

To be alone, absolutely alone, is to no longer try to justify yourself to other men: silence is the precondition for entering the land of the dead. No one crosses the border talking. The land of the dead co-exists with the world of the living, not side-by-side, but interpenetrating; it remains invisible to the community of men and is driven away by conversational chatter as if by prayer or static interference forming voids impossible to cross. To be alone is to see. This is what we see: We are constantly being fed upon by invisible phantoms. These phantoms are the homicidal desires of others, murderous demons cast out by denial and repression and self-delusion. We are connected by murder—networks of homicide. Each proclamation of personal innocence creates such a shadow demon. Each inner justification breeds a vampiric double-phantom. It is impossible to live in the ordinary sense of the term, ie. among others, without breeding demons. I have counted 111 demons. Most human beings are nothing more than a virulent locus for the throwing off of demons. They decompose in demons. They are a cistern of phantoms. There is no cure for this situation. Psychoanalysis and other forms of "therapy," television, magazines, newspapers, film, etc. are all techniques of self-induced hypnosis—a communal hive-hum. To live among others is to be distracted from the slaughterhouse. For this reason, isolation often leads to what is perceived as madness. One behaves, after all, in a certain incomprehensible way when one is traversing a battlefield no one else perceives. The forbidden only appears to the man who has transgressed all laws: and the greatest of these laws is a basic belief in the human and the value of life. Up until now, even the greatest transgressors have JUSTIFIED themselves. They have sought the understanding of their fellow men, if not those of their own time, then those of some imagined future. Madmen are often recycled as prophets. In that, they've still obeyed the Law. They haven't dared the Great Transgression: to be forever isolated, forever misunderstood, to see and proclaim what can never be proven. The torment of the great transgressor is not only that he cannot communicate, but that he will not communicate. To communicate leaves everything unsaid. Dust fills the throat, a knot of maggots. The tongue is eaten to the root. The jaw thrown open, packed with orange mud. Nothing ever comes back from the land of the dead. All lines of communication break down between here and there. The torment of the great transgressor is also his ecstasy: it is his passport beyond the border. He's sworn to secrecy. This is all he can say and it is not enough: **THEY EXIST**. *"He may find himself beset by larval beings, desperate to be observed and to exist by being observed." —Wm. S. Burroughs.* I listen to the ocean, not the real ocean, that doesn't exist anymore. No, I'm listening to the ocean that whooshes through my earphones, the digital ocean, that never changes, the white noise that will always be there. The oceanic confusion. Whoosh, it goes. Whoosh. When I play my private ocean, it's like I'm drowning, or have already drowned, well-passed the point where you struggle any longer, where instead you've accepted that you'll never reach the surface. I'm lying face-up under the water and looking out at the faces of everyone else looking down, mouths mouthing empty words, I can't hear a word they're saying, blessedly. This is baptism, this is salvation. I'm separated from their world and vice versa by a dividing line that cannot be crossed: the surface. That's what its like, I imagine, to experience suicide by drowning. I remember hearing, from some source I considered reliable at the time but that I cannot remember at the moment, that of all the methods to commit suicide, drowning is not too bad a choice. If, I suppose, you can get past the panic and instinctual fear, the frantic urge to struggle to the surface, to cry for help, to gulp for air. Not many can. You're advised to redirect the same natural urge you have to cry out for help to pull in as much water as you can, filling your lungs with liquid, which is, according to this same source I cannot remember, a sensation supposedly rather pleasant, relatively speaking. *I have something to say but I lack the breath, the atmosphere, in which to say it.* So is freezing to death. Supposed to be pleasant, that is. But it's not always feasible to freeze to death and that, too, has its uncomfortable aspects, the shivering, the chattering, the pain in the extremities before the numbness claims dominion, the possibility of discovery, etc. You don't want to be discovered.

Cut to a coffee shop, Seventh Avenue: it's a Saturday night, hours before the riots break out, the gunfire, the executions, the wholesale rape and slaughter. I'm sitting by a window near a subway entrance, drinking a paper cup of coffee; it's important to keep awake. If they catch you sleeping, you're finished. Pigeons pecking at the smear your eyeball leaves on the early-morning pavement. The rest of you, twisted, like a torn-up old coat full of abortions and slaughterhouse offal. That's all they'll find of you when the sun comes up. Hosing it off the sidewalk into the gutter. If you must sleep, find a steel cocoon somewhere. It's cold tonight, twenty-five degrees, even colder in the wind. Wind-chill. ::Are you dead yet?:: She asks him this impatiently. She's dressed for the evening: a little black cocktease dress, black heels, something formal, or, maybe, intimate, it's all the same in this case. She checks her watch, the square face surrounded by diamonds. An old anniversary gift? She pouts. ::Fucking asshole, do you have to be such a stubborn prick about everything?:: He's lying face-down, naked, the mattress already soaked with urine. Around his head, the plastic bag, held tightly round his throat with a thick elastic band reinforced by duct tape, smears his features into an anonymous goo. A.k.a: nothing. The muscle paralyzer she administered earlier makes him so lazy and uncoordinated its impossible for him to complete the simple task of reaching up and pulling off the death mask. His death, though, it coming slow, slow, slow. ::I'm having an affair, you worthless prick. I want you to know." She prods him in the side with a rolled up Vogue. ::Did you hear me, asshole? Haven't you got anything to say about that?:: His lips move under the plastic, like a pulpated slug, but nothing comes out, just a smear of bubbling drool pressed under the plastic. ::Christ, how pathetic.:: Minutes pass. Out of sheer anxiety and an irrational spurt of typical marital anger, certain that he's suffocating slowly *on purpose,* out of fucking spite

the selfish bastard, she petulantly shoves a good portion of her hair
dryer up his ass. ::There:: she says, apropos of nothing, and,
somehow relieved, she laughs, setting the blast on high. At the
terminal, watching the departure board: it wipes black and reposts the
times, but all the posted times are "impossible," the trains leaving
before they're even supposed to be there, and vice versa, everyone
waiting, numb, somnolent, passive, faces upturned, and the board is
updated in this fashion again and again, before blacking out
altogether: no trains, in other words, are coming or leaving
necropolis. Armed guards standing at all the gates, ominously
anonymous as insects in gas masks, dripping with emergency gear,
absolutely no one allowed on the platforms, no exceptions, shoot-to-
kill. A pretty Asian girl, tank top, soft round belly playing peek-a-boo
above tight, faded jeans takes a picture of herself with a disposable
camera. Flash-flash. In a smear of blood, four teeth on the dirty
linoleum floor: the scene, more likely than not, of an impromptu
interrogation. Let's everyone move on. Nothing here to see. "*Each
page is a door to everything is permitted*," says Wm. S. Burroughs. A large
room, like a ward, functional pallets on rollers, and lying on each, a
naked man. Each man is being masturbated by his wife or girlfriend,
and, in a few cases, a mother or sister. The men appear to be
drugged, or otherwise tranquilized; perhaps they've been erotically
hypnotized into a rosy compliance. This is the way it's done, the
harvesting of energy. The general idea is that when they shoot their
load into a waiting receptacle they will be simultaneously killed.
Presumably the collected "death seed" is a kind of magickal delicacy,
as well as a gourmand specialty at high-end dinner parties, and it has
great importance for the ongoing eugenic program. In any event, the
female who sacrifices her male in this way is entitled to a large cash
award, legal immunity, and a place in good standing with the BWS, or
Black Widow Society. ::It shows a certain admirable power, you see,::
says the recruiting officer, ::to erotically coax a man to death. We
need women like that in the Society. Many benefits are accrued by
the talented Widow.:: Throughout the room, the naked men are
groaning and writhing in various states of sexual excitement. At their
sides, the women have been encouraged to "pray"—in other words,

to whisper the special sex fantasy they know will send their boy to heaven. With the women erotically costumed, or simply half-naked, the scene resembles an orgy in a hospital ICU, or a pornographic Golgotha without all the crosses: *pornocalypse*. One wife, in fishnets and micro-mini, tits bare, interrupts her intimately whispered glossolalia about strap-on dildos, electricity, and toe-sucking, and motions with a free hand to an attendant with the lethal syringe. Ah, the sting of Death. The other hand slows down to a maintenance rhythm on her husband's engorged cock. ::Mine's cumming:: she squeals, genuinely excited, waving more frantically. ::Over here! Oh…hurry, hurry!:: Swift and silent as a black shark, the attendant slips to the side of the gurney and injects the now laboring man ((up, Up he climbs towards clear-headed ecstasy, Father, Father, I commend my spirit into your hands)) in the ankle. The distillation of various snake, insect, and sea-creature venoms combined with erection enhancing drugs race through his circulatory system burning everything along the way and hit his brain like an erotic jackhammer. The attendant Widow recedes quietly with her empty stinger and leaves the wife to her final moments of tender intimacies with hubby. Her hand, still holding his cock, as he convulses, drools, farts, and stiffens, he is transfigured in sexual agony for a few unbearable seconds, finally spurting like he's squeezing it out of hell itself, jetting his creamy death-milk into the receptacle. ::Oh honey…:: she gasps, ::Oh…oh…honey! Oh Goddess, YES!:: She spontaneously orgasms, simultaneously, her soaking cunt grasping nothing, she's completely unashamed, a Virgin Mary. Snow. Lying on a pile of cold bodies, a cold body myself, I see, as if through a microscope, a single snow-flake land on the smooth buttocks under my cheek: it doesn't melt. Flies, looking sexual, rub their forelegs together in anticipation of the feast. Shit, or everything turning into it. Hospital room: why does the man on the bed, eaten away by some variety of nameless cancer, ((a host of carnivorous ghosts)), dying, keep his gold-digging wife around? She sits in his room bored, impatient, distracted. She checks her watch. Lunch with Ted at one. Maybe he's running a sex/death fantasy no one knows about, not even her, not even him. *La belle dame sans merci*. Holding up his head, ::Look at your toes, love, aren't

they adorable? I painted them while you were in the recovery room.
Oh, and by the way, they removed your kidney this time.:: The rumor
is that a secret consortium of billionaires is sponsoring a think-tank
of scientists, theologians, philosophers, engineers, etc—an operation
on the scale and scope of the Manhattan Project—whose purpose
seems to be the construction of (unbelievably enough) an Archangel.
The purpose? It seems that the intent is to produce a weapon capable
of doing battle with monstrosity. **Woman: An obsolete machine**
Unconscious Her: Out of fear and misplaced orgasm desire, there arises
an institution of gender slavery: a man's self-fictional envy
(submission strategy) to pay (false) homage to a woman's ability to
conceive and bear a child. We'll never be complicit in this species
propagation propaganda—this infestation (of locusts, of death). We
have no cunt envy: the supposed mystery and fascination of a
woman's reproductive potential is null and void for two reasons: 1)
We don't consider bearing a child to be anything but an enormous
ethical, tactical, and aesthetic error. To deliver a child is a catastrophe,
a plague, a participation in holocaust—a concession to the slime
flood of evolution which is a tide of imprisonment and a leakage that
bears almost infinite plague pustules, spores of conservation, sham
evolution. Woman is a conservative engine. It's ludicrous to applaud
an event that is nothing but a capitulation to suffering and an
unthinking xerox-machine-repetition of the same mistake out of
sheer docility, laziness, selfishness, and stupidity—and more: a lack of
anti-anthropomorphic courage. 2) There is, obviously, nothing a
woman has to "do" to conceive and "have" a child: it's simply a
process that occurs, like developing lymphoma or cataracts. Abortion
and condoms are the cure for this disease, a shield for outer space
disasters. The old dichotomy: a woman is—and a man does. To birth
a child is no more meritorious than having a bowel movement—and
it's just about as infantile to take pride in such an anti-event, the
egotistical self-enchantment of our bodily excretions. Biological
byproducts (waste materiel) forms itself in the body's cavity and nine
months later one involuntarily collapses with internal paroxysm and
produces a howling shit. *Woman is infantile* and the infant is her
egomaniacal dwarf-double, her Mini-me. Women can create nothing

but themselves. It's not the penis women envy but a man's ability to create/escape: woman is rooted below the hips in dirt. Her toes clutch roots. Chronology be damned: a woman bears a child out of fury, and she delivers it out of revenge: the act is a pale simulacra of a man's capacity for true creation, auto-generation, out of nothing. *We must not let Him escape!* "Our Father, who art in Heaven, etc." Men create what has not existed—they create what is extra-aneous of simple survival economy. Men open an aperture, a true cunt, in the possible to allow the impossible to enter. Men are the conceivers of the after-human and the vital trajectory of blast-off is grooved along the fantasies and suppressed energy of their sperm flow. *Woman is an obsolete machine.* She's been unnecessary for thousands of years. Man must unseal his cunt, fertilize himself, self-fuck, true immaculate conception: he must give birth to what's next. **afterhuman.**
ILLINGTON, N.C. (December 30) — A woman attacked a man, targeting his genitals during a Christmas party, injuring him badly enough that he needed 50 stitches, authorities said Friday. Rebecca Arnold Dawson, 34, was charged with malicious castration in a fight early Tuesday at a party hosted by the 38-year-old man's girlfriend, police said. Ms. Dawson is accused of grabbing the man's genitals. Police said a weapon was not used. A police spokesperson declined to elaborate. "I believe he needed more than 50 stitches to repair the damage, but he is back home at this point," the spokesperson said. "All we can tell you is that the injury was done with her hands." Dawson does not have a listed phone number. State law describes malicious castration as cutting off, maiming or disfiguring a person's genitals with the intent to hurt or render the victim impotent.

::Every time we get started, sir, something compromises the experiment and we have to destroy everything we've done and start all over again. What I mean to say, sir, is something gets *inside*. We can't keep the area uncontaminated no matter what precautions we take. It's non-local, discontinuous, everywhere we look and everywhere at once...as if it were in the very nature of things, as if it were synonymous with...well, looking itself, with *everything*.:: The snow falls softer, quicker, hushing the city, making it easier for

assassins to slip from scene to scene: a shadow behind the flakes just
out of sight. You feel the crosshairs clutching at you like an old
heartbreak. A silent shot: you fall. ::*I can see you at your desk dreamily
running your tongue across your slightly swollen upper lip where I'd bitten you.
Owned! And, oh, your pretty feet! Biting the soft soles of your feet before I rub
them against me, spilling my warm, creamy cum on your toes, painted like little
jewels. I was thinking of you feeling your bitten bottom when you sat down at
work, or the delicious little pain when someone brushes past your sore-bitten titties
in the elevator....::* In the waiting room, waiting. The nurse stands in the
hallway like a ghost. She holds a clipboard and calls your name.
You get up to follow and she vanishes into the chilled air. Long pale
yellow corridors opening into empty rooms. You are alone. Each
room equipped with the identical instruments for probing and
evaluating submissive human bodies: collection tubes, dials calibrated
to measure pain, swabs, hammers, probes, glittering steel tools. All of
it inscrutable: torture. The ubiquitous examination table with its
crinkly disposable white paper to absorb leakage, changed after each
diagnosis. On the counter, a tube of surgical lubricant. Something
violently splashed into the bottom of the archetypal stainless steel
sink: a thin, milky liquid with shreds. You sit there, waiting. Bare toes
dangling over the linoleum floor, hairy thighs parted, penis shriveled
in its dark nest. ::Anything can happen,:: Dr. Parker says, talking
about the uncertainties of the interior. We are labyrinths inside, he
implies, and death can hide anywhere. You shoot a man in the
stomach, or cut him open with a razor, and his labyrinth spills out.
::It's a minor operation,:: she tells him, tracing a red nail along his
shaved scrotum. ::They cut here and slip them out. You'll be so much
happier this way, honey. We both will.:: Cut to: several photographs
of a middle-aged man, different angles, propped on elbows and
knees, dressed in a thin pink chemise and thong sandals with two-
inch heels. His cock is jammed into a sexy high-heeled sandal, the
twisted cross-straps, decorated with a small black leather bow,
positioned just behind the swollen pink head. He is licking a picture
of his wife's pretty bare feet on the laptop screen in front of this face.
The man has, apparently, been entirely habituated to this scene. ::It's
all perfectly normal. We lead men in this direction every day.:: says

the prim specialist, hair like a lacquered honeycomb. Monstrosity: somewhere inside the labyrinth, its lurking, a shadowy presence, slipping inside a fold of intestinal flesh. --the heart speeds up, there are marked increases in respiration and blood-pressure, the adrenal glands are squirting. Suddenly, you're a nervous wreck, sick, dizzy, paranoid, a free-floating feeling of doom pervading everything: it's *monstrosity* that has slipped unseen into room. You want to run, but there's nowhere to run. It's as if you were being followed by a UFO with a thousand eyes slow-tracking you from above the earth's atmosphere. Impossible, everyone says. You are suffering from an illusion. ::It's not in the room you see:: the doctor explains, ::its living inside you. You're carrying. Do you understand?:: Monstrosity passing over your brain like the shadow of some tentacled thing, fear-itself, like a flying extra-dimensional vampiric octopus. *Do you understand?* ::No, doctor, I don't understand.:: He smiles, taps his forehead, ::Ah but you see, that's just the thing. You aren't supposed to understand.::

A small gathering in a mausoleum for the funeral of the family matriarch, dead, at 77, of Alzheimer's. Thank God. The minister babbling the usual: the promise of reincarnation, the spiritual body, eternal life, etc, all the bad logic and bald lies. Everyone pretending to pay attention so hard they miss the trembling of the white and pink tulips on the casket. Soon, though, the trembling grows so pronounced a few spot it. There's a wind howling outside: maybe there's a draft? *Out of the corpse rises a bloodthirsty spirit which takes possession of the living. The power to murder one of our own kind is felt inwardly as a supreme power, a diving power." –Alphonso Lingis* The minister continues: something about Jesus coming in the twinkling of an eye, when you least expect it, He's here! He's here!, the resurrection is at hand. We've heard all this before; it's vaguely comforting, like a lullaby you don't need to pay attention to. There's a knocking sound coming from the casket now. Everyone tries to ignore it at first, but it's growing embarrassingly loud. The minister clears his throat and tries talking above it. Some coughing in the congregation. Maybe there's an airplane or a train passing nearby. Certainly it can't be vermin? The flowers slip off the top of the casket and the whole damn thing is shaking. "Oh my god!" several mourners shout. Old women drop in a dead faint. Terror paralyzes others. Maybe it's an earthquake. It occurs to someone: "GET HER OUT OF THERE. SHE'S ALIVE!" Someone else rushes to the trembling coffin. It's unnecessary. The sides splinter and the lid explodes and the old woman sits stock upright in a shower of sawdust. Screams. Obscenities. Chairs overturn. The minister drops his Bible like a five-hundred-pound black brick and backs away clutching his chest, jaw dropping like a horse-skull in the desert. Speechless. People shrieking, sobbing, praying. The old lady looks around angrily, mouth furiously working, nothing coming out. No one notices that the walls of the tombs around them are *vibrating*. The seals around each internment have broken and the dead are pushing out the slabs. They're crawling out from inside, bones and knotted cloth and black flesh all held together by bits of shriveled tendon. This is the Resurrection: but it doesn't look like anything painted by the Italian masters. It looks more like something directed by George A. Romero. No one recognizes it. But this is what Jesus promised us. This is what we've been waiting for. **This is Eternal Life!** The good news is coming over the radios across the country: the dead have risen! Then come the reports of a family brutally slaughtered in the remodeled kitchen of their suburban Maplewood home. A woman pulled out of her car at an intersection Oak and Freeley and eaten alive. A subway car of commuters dismembered and eviscerated on the R-line. The dead have taken over an entire office building in midtown. The police are fighting them floor by floor in a frantic search for survivors. The death-toll, unofficially, already stands at 2,850. The long dark night of the toilet hole... *"The void frees me from what attaches me. In the void there is nowhere to stop. Creating the void ahead of me, I immediately sense the beloved there—where there is nothing. What was I desperately in love with? A glimpse, an open door."* –Georges Bataille They are lying in bed together, candlelight all around, and she tells him what she's in the mood for. ::Suki, momma wants a bite of your tittie.:: Kneeling, he holds a pale tittie to her lips. ::Suki, momma wants to taste your toes tonite.:: He obediently holds up a delicately painted foot to be bitten. ::Lipstick and little bite marks all over you chest, tummy, thighs and bottom, you luscious little sissypet:: It's a sunny afternoon, mild, after so many frozen days, and you begin to feel like meat again, like something for which something else, completely alien, like a thousand years of death, hungers. Something slips loose inside the eye, a fragment, a little sliver of pupil. In the mirror, you see your own asshole, star-shaped, or fungoid, something clutching at you, like a black parasite. But, by now, it can't be removed. Solar anus: it shits on us from god. The old fortune-teller, blind, eyes like puckered assholes, fungoid, parasites sucking the brains from her skull, and the side-effect is that she can see: ::You must go on a godyssey.:: Antonin Artaud says, *"The force that builds up tidal waves, that makes the sea lap at the moon, that has lava rising from the depths of volcanoes; the force that shakes buildings and creates deserts; the force red and unpredictable that sends thoughts like so many crimes seething through our heads, and crimes innumerable, like lice; the force that supports and aborts life—these are concrete manifestations of an energy whose heavier aspect is the Sun."* What he means is this: One morning, just like any other. As she reads a magazine at the kitchen table, strange hands, my hands, mould themselves over her delicate shoulders, intelligent thumbs probing all the empty spaces between her vertebrae, the discontinuity of her, the alienness, the other. ::That feels good:: she says. Her hair smells warm, like cake, or maybe, it's her brains thinking up plots to destroy me. I burrow my nose into the clean white part in her hair. She turns a page. My penis hardens against her spine, which is like a buried cable, and I feel countless messages running back and forth, a riot of communication, but from and to whom? She closes her eyes, slumping forward, as if. As if. My hands run casually up along her shoulders, like a caress, like a, no, it really is like a caress. Flash bulbs pop! Pop, pop. Poppity-pop! Behind her eyes, she sees herself dead in a crime-scene photo: body sprawled on the floor beside the table, sweatpants stained at the crotch, one black Chinese slipper fallen off, bare toes clenched. I yank her head violently to the side and smile over her shoulder at the digital camera I've hidden in the fireplace. Her body, pale and small, humped up on the kitchen table, sweatpants now yanked down, ass exposed. Dogs, birds, niggers, neighbors wander in and fuck her, roots of trees, rain, the moon fucks her, a thousand stars and the icy cold penetrate her, moles, voles, rats, and larvae fuck her, everything invading her , her back door open, the house itself fucks her as it collapses, as centuries pass, weather and radio broadcasts and the countless dead swarming all over the raw white meat of her fuck her. Death: to be raped by infinity. *"When you have managed to penetrate a certain kind of hatred, it's then that you truly feel love." –Antonin Artaud* Oh, Antonin. Hatred is a frontier. A boundary. A godyssey of a thousand light-years begins with a single murder. But who should you kill? Because I can't kill everyone, do I end up killing no one at all?

From now on, I'll treat her like I'd treat a stranger, which is what she is, which is what everyone is: one of the alien undead. I'll treat her with a distant politeness, hand on the stun-gun, as I treat anyone else. She's unpredictable and lethal, like all zombies: HANDLE WITH CARE! The goal: not to get stung, bitten, clawed, or sprayed with stink, not to be turned into one of THEM. She's such a self-justifying, toxic, judgmental, obfuscating, autocratic creature form another dimension---exuding, like a staining indelible ink, an obfuscating blame in all directions save the center, the center, of course, being herself. Disgust, hard to believe I feel it for her, too, my beloved, but I do: like a mutant octopus, pale, sickly, membranous blue, an organ bag with all manner of cancerous parasitic squirming inside: *monstrosity*. That's what love is: monstrosity. That's what love is, shambling towards you over the barren plain, alien zombies with a hunger for your entrails, ready to redden their teeth with you, but wearing a false-face over a face like a plate of maggots, a sweet mask that smiles and whispers ::Come here, my love, my darling, I want to kiss you.:: It's best to walk forward, to walk through the world as if you were walking through an asylum of dangerous lunatics, trying to understand the mania of the inmates, if only to cajole, to deflect, to emerge from the ward at the end of the day with your body and sanity intact, if not, that is, to do "good," like Jesus, for which he was crucified. All I have left of my beloved, I

carry in my pocket like sacred relics through this asylum, this
pornocalyptic wasteland: it's an incomplete collection of seventeen
nails, each lacquered red, left behind from her fingers and toes.
That's all that's left of my love. That's enough magic to ward off the
dead forever. *BAKERSFIELD, Calif. (March 4) - A couple's plans for a
birthday party for their former pet chimpanzee turned tragic when two other
chimps at an animal sanctuary escaped from their cage and attacked. The man
was critically injured with massive wounds to his face, body and limbs, and the
attacking animals were shot dead. The couple had brought Moe a cake and were
standing outside his cage when Buddy and Ollie, two of four chimpanzees in the
adjoining cage, attacked St. James Davis. LaDonna Davis, 64, suffered a bite
wound to the hand while trying to help her 62-year-old husband. St. James Davis
had severe facial injuries and would require extensive surgery in an attempt to
reattach his nose, Dr. Maureen Martin of Kern Medical Center told KGET-TV
of Bakersfield. His testicles and a foot also were severed. Buddy, a 16-year-old
male chimp, initiated the attack and after he was shot, Ollie, a 13-year-old male,
grabbed the gravely injured man and dragged him down the road, authorities said.*

It's the day of personal apocalypse: Apocalypse I. The dead speak an
alien language—a hungry gibberish. Language is the sound
mastication makes without the food. Behind a Starbucks counter, a
sweet-faced Asian clerk takes your order, but if you listen closely to
her lisping pipsqueak voice, you can hear the squishy lump of your
pancreas smashed to pale goo between her teeth. Two woman oil the
pretty toes of a corpse they are about to cook in a preheated oven.
The corpse's toes look just like the toes of the wife of the man sitting
on the couch watching this scene on a laptop computer, pumping his
cock, and praying with his eyes rolled back in his head ::Oh look at
you now you bitch, oh look at you now, dead, with a banana stuffed
in your cunt and a meat thermometer rammed in your ass, what are
you going to do now, you bitch…huh…what are you going to do
now. I bet you never saw this coming?:: At the Apocalypse I it's not
necessary that anyone else sees that the world has ended: at the point
of personal omega, no other points-of-view exist. Others are like
curling wisps of smoke, empty pods, dry sticks, walking dust-piles; in

accordance with zombie film philosophy, they can only hurt you if you believe in them. Believe…in who? There's no one here but I…and whoever I'm talking to, whoever understands my language, whoever hears my scream on this windless lunar plain. Who is no one. No one hears me. No one is here. I am here and this is the Apocalypse. The original sin is dialogue. To say that I am god is to say nothing but that I was born, that I died, and, because I'm here in the first place, that I must, of necessity, have risen again. I am Jesus, of course, as if you didn't know that already. But here's a revelation: I am also monstrosity.

All is one. All is monstrosity. This text is sin. Apocalypse is just a special way of looking at the world: any day can be the last day. It's a matter of perspective and suddenly you can see the otherlands open up before you. Ask a suicide, or a spree-killer, or a man crucified in a hospital bed… Landscape of meat and lightning…We carry our apocalypse inside us like a gene we've carried all our lives that one day *turns on.*

Meet the god coming towards you from the other side of the mirror. …and then shatter the mirror. *"The man with the axe is your friend and equal. He will come, a brutal man, who will lift you out of tiredness."* --The Epic of Gilgamesh You break off all communication; you cut the incoming lines. Everything's down. Clouds of static, venomous man'o'wars drift over the western landscape. Imagine dead roots in a hard dry soil. No rain, *for millennia.* You leave only one line operational: the line out. This is the line that carries your broadcast over the cracked and arid wasteland, a rambling monologue of insane ranting and exhortation that's heard, if at all, in fragments hacked apart by electrical storms. The man in the high tower, the bunker, the crypt…He surveys the empty landscape. ::I am a hunter on the trail of love.:: That speck, over there. Telescopic sight.

"There are those who will maintain that the schizo is incapable of uttering the word 'I,' and that we must restore his ability to pronounce this hallowed word. All of which the schizo sums up by saying: they're fucking me over again." –Gilles Deleuze and Felix Guattari My dreams are populated by the assassin-doubles of all those who haven't been able to kill me when awake: drinking my life-force, they slip under the defenses by becoming indistinguishable from my own thoughts, as in all energy being one, all thought becomes one thought, an invisible broadcast. Mind-control. The other becomes me: I sympathize with Them. When you begin to *understand* your enemy, you're already defeated. When borders become porous, definition is lost, and all becomes a homogeneous, undifferentiated, half-digested porridge: a kind of basic energy core, a cancer-mass, a monstrosity. The dream is a malignancy of labyrinths, ever-expanding from the center, the I, into which you're thrust, lost, a place of utter isolation, whose reality obliterates the consensual lie we agree to mistake for "life," and which you're obliged to wander inside search of an exit. There is no exit. *"Let us leave textual criticism to graduate students, formal criticism to aesthetes, and recognize that what has been said is not still to be said; that an expression does not have the same value twice, does not live two lives; that all words, once spoken, are dead and function only at the moment when they are uttered, that a form once it has served, cannot be used again and asks only to be replaced by another." --Antonin Artaud* On the bed your lover lies, a silver patch of slime on her thigh, a few pubic hairs matted flat and stuck there. When she shifts, slightly, to reach for the TV remote, you see the glistening mucky darkness at the center of her. ::You see, it's a genetic defect we've engineered to pass on the plague and create more victims simultaneously. Quite ingenious really. They're programmed to respond to produce their own self-destruction: when they see those tits, those asses, those toes. Smell those glandular secretions. A female, for instance, on her belly, head propped on her hands, legs bent at the knees, ankles crossed, the soles of the feet exposed…when they see that *hole* they cant resist sticking it in.:: The reporter scribbles away on his pad. This, his instincts tell him, is the *good stuff.* If he can only keep the old boy talking. On the record, off the record, what's the difference? If it sticks to the wall. ::So, Herr

Doktor, the female of the species, you are saying that she is the root of all evil, then? You can't possibly mean that?:: Chuckling, the old alien responds ::Female of the species? Surely you jest, sir.:: ::What do you mean?:: ::Why my good fellow, there is no 'female' of the species.:: The writer stops writing for a moment. He looks up. The alien's face pointed, inquisitive, insectoid in spite of the false-face. ::But all those billboards, magazine covers, movie posters:: ::Precisely! Simulacrum, of course. Pure imagination. Propaganda. They never existed:: ::Women are an illusion? Literally?:: The reporter, shaken, knows he should be writing but cannot. Writer's block. The alien grins slyly through his human mask, savoring this perverse exposure of his obscene machinations. Apparently, creators, in whatever dimension they inhabit, sooner or later hunger for an audience. Comedians and murderers, too. Exhibitionists all. If there were a God, you could bet your balls he'd step forward to claim credit. Everyone wants to show their private parts. ::It's true, then. Women are evil, designed for evil? Just like the Old Testament and all those insane, misogynistic desert saints said they were? And after all these years of de-conditioning. Reindoctrination. That's outrageous.:: The writer takes a private moment to reflect on the tragedy of all the time, emotion, energy, money, etc., wasted in pursuit of creatures that never existed. When he surfaces again, he says, with bitterness, ::They're soulless then. Mere automata.:: The alien's face crinkles and collapses in delight. Irony, deception, and betrayal are evidently what activates its pleasure centers. That's what makes it "alien." But then is it really so. Alien? He provides a few potent synonyms. ::An illusion, a trap, a detour to nowhere.:: The writer returns his pen to his pad with a vengeance. He scribbles notes as he talks. ::That means only the male of the species exists?:: ::Well, if there's no 'female' does it really make any sense to say the 'male' of the species?:: The alien waits in lip-smacking anticipation for this tidbit to sink in. It takes a while. Humans are notoriously slow. The writer looks up from his hieroglyphic scrawl. ::My god, you mean the gender wars are completely fabricated?:: It's almost too much for the old alien. He really should take it easy at his age, all those light-years crossed, it's not easy, not even on the immortal. This kind of pleasure will surely annihilate him one of these days, but he cant help it: "enlightening" these naïve minors just feels so ferociously *good.* His voice is a digital hum filled with the nihilistic sound of clicking beetles and dead-end codes. ::All fake, all fake, all fake. You've been shooting yourselves in your own asses, metaphorically, and literally, speaking, for millennia. You've got to admit, it's all very comical from a certain perspective. The universe is not without a sense of humor:: ::I guess it *is* amusing,:: the writer concedes, but drily, ::if you're far enough away from it. Like in another dimension maybe.:: The alien winks, mimes a "shooting" movement with his fingers and clicks his tongue. ::You got it, baby.:: ::But why? Why do it?:: The alien shrugs, tired now of this conversation, tired of this human, of all humans, the way you're tired of a whore when you're done with her and she's tired of you the moment you're all paid up. A mutual weariness. ::Why— that's such a prototypically *human* question. The question you really should be asking yourself is, Why not?:: I like thinking of ways of making you talk as if you weren't any older than a toddler. Sometimes I imagine constant reinforcement of baby-talk until it becomes natural. I might slap you if you use your grown up voice, or only respond to you when you express yourself like my baby suki. I think that's more exciting and rewarding than just hypnotizing you because I like seeing you gradually lose the ability or willingness to "use your words". Sometimes I like to think of giving you medicine that slowly dulls your ability to speak (I like that one a lot). Sometimes I think of paralyzing your tongue and having your teeth gently removed or filed down til they look like baby teeth.

WAYNESVILLE, N.C. (March 16)- Three men accused of operating what police described as a sadomasochistic "dungeon" that included castrations have been sentenced to jail time. Richard Peter "Master Rick" Sciara, his partner of 20 years Michael Mendez, and the man they called their slave, Danny Carroll Reeves, pleaded guilty to felony castration and maiming. Superior Court Judge Dennis Winner said it was difficult to call the dungeon's willing patients "victims," but he said six castrations performed there were certainly a crime. "I think this is a type of perversion that cannot be tolerated by society," Winner said during a sentencing hearing Thursday. Prosecutors said the men ran a sadomasochistic "dungeon" fashioned from an enclosed carport in 2004 and 2005 at a house in a quiet neighborhood near Waynesville in western North Carolina. Six men, some from as far away as South America, came to the home for castration, while others went seeking other types of body-modification surgery, prosecutors said.

Woman: a non-existent machine. *AUTO-FANTASY:* we fuck ourselves. Woman is a man's projection onto a void (whether or not a man is likewise a woman's projection onto a void doesn't concern us at the moment, or ever, and why should it, as soon will be evident if not evident already.) Man—always alone, and properly so: stripped to dreaming. He lies on a bed, fantasizing, jerking off—or cock buried in a vagina, fucking nothing but imagination. Only a man knows what he desires. He constructs his desire-fulfilling machine to satisfy these desires but it is not a woman that satisfies these desires. Woman is a clumsy strategy for her own survival and survival of the species through the xerox of her genetic material and the captured genetic material of a chosen male. Woman is a dumb (dump) process at the beginning of an assembly line: baby, baby, baby, baby… (i.e. an obsolete machine). She mimics the male desire-fullfilling machine, but she is not this male desire-fulfilling machine. *INTERNET COMMUNICATION:* desire without bodies—man is able to create his desire fulfilling machine in real-time which is no time, being the non-existent "now" (i.e. Eternity, angelic-fuck). Man constructs his own desire-fulfilling machine, fleshless, without body, not stuck in space. Man, free of time and space, free of woman. The tools at "hand," finally, to create the perfect desire-fulfilling machine (Angel). After four years cyber experimentation it's conclusive: no one makes a better woman than a man. Woman, stripped of flesh--and the biological species xerox machine concealed inside—reveals herself as nullity, an awkward series of gestures, bad mimesis, only a tracing of the kind of machine that fulfills man's desire. Her conviction that it is enough to simply "be," rather than "do," that only her simple animal-machine presence justifies her existence, makes her a virtual non-entity in a virtual world. The strategy of false-mystification is broken in binary. X-ray vision—seeing through the flesh, one sees the inner workings and the "workings" of woman are non-existent outside of a simple duplication and mimetic machine. Woman is an emptiness—flesh spread on super-specialized plumbing. *FAKE GIRLS:* transexuals, transgendered machines, cyberchicks, cyborgs, dolls, man-ikins. The immanence of man's first fully functional desire-fullfilling machines: total sex, zero conception, true love—anti-biology, anti-septic, anti-human. Solo-erotic. It's now possible to break the pussy barrier: to free oneself of the yin-yang gravitational field. The revelation that breaks a man's self-hypnotic biological dependence-gaze on women, on the vampirism that drains the imaginative and seminal fuels necessary for blast-off (angelic fuck, penetration of Impossible, aperture, laceration, opening of unisexual cosmic cunt), beyond the conventional, the economic, all the caveman survival strategies: the evolutionary leap to a different level, spark—vistas, visions, mutations, assemblages, collisions. Woman is not only an obsolete machine. *Woman is a non-existent machine.*

To sum up: There is no such thing as woman. Man has fictionalized woman out of his own desire. Man=Woman. But Woman does not equal Man. Man doesn't just contain, project the feminine. He *is* the feminine. The bioform, flesh-machine, cellular engine known as "woman" is no longer a necessity—or a desirability—as reproduction is no longer necessary or desirable. It is a liability.
(Extinction/orgasm) The well-guarded secret. Man, awakening, from blindness, bedazzlement, enslavement, self-enchantment, eroto-somnolence, alimony, palimony, child-support, life-support—the survival stupidities employed by non-existent obsolete machines. Woman as black hole, constant drain, trickle-down-economy-waste. (Woman obsolete even in her non-existence/non-existent even in her obsolescence). The end of pro-Creation. Flash future: These machines stand empty, isolated, out of fuel on barren fields. Useless, abandoned, unable to fix themselves. (Rubber, glue, silicon, surgical staples: the plastic surgeons abandon the project and become desert prophets proclaiming the new Whore-Messiah). These machines invented and once fueled by men's dreams. Built by men, serviced by

men, loved by men, worshipped by men: Ruins. Indecipherable crude technologies unrecognized by what follows. *Afterhuman*.

Out here, bwana, it's kill or be killed. I'd like to think that I'm an undercover agent, a double-agent, a triple-agent, no doubt, maybe even a rogue agent, but for who, or what? Frankly, we've lost track. People are dangerous and it doesn't hurt to be courteous to them, and by "courteous" I mean "cautious." That's all courtesy is, really, a ceremonial form of caution. Cities are nothing but paradigm grids laid down over vast anarchic alien hunting grounds—a stage-set, basically, for an all-out killing field, a slaughterzone. It's clear that I'm betraying them—these so-called "humans," or exposing them: it's the same thing, really. But it's not clear who I'd be betraying them to. Is there anyone left to betray anyone to? If there's no one to betray them to, then what's the point? Indeed, what's the point of anything? I've been asking myself precisely that question for years. Without answer, I hardly need to add. You can't betray someone to no one. Okay, agreed. You can't expose someone if there's no one to see the truth. You can't bring someone to justice in an environment without government, that is without justice. All I can do is to say *"I see you. I know what you are,"* and fat lot of good that'll do me, except to mark myself out, to become the target of all their hostility, of their engines of self-protection, their concentration camps, their hospitals, their newspapers, their execution squads, their persecution complexes. ::You're mad, you know:: ::Quite::

Time to go… *"We are apparently confronted with such a radical nullity that, in the exorbitance it represents, the danger of which it is the approach, the tension it provokes, it demands, as if it were the price to be freed from it, the formulation of an initial word which would banish all the words which say something."* —*Maurice Blanchot* What is that initial word of which the prophet speaks? If I could speak it, the world would instantaneously collapse, like an asshole closing around a withdrawing endoscope. Every sentence I write is a futile search to find the one word that will assassinate the world. Maurice Blanchot also asks, "Could suffering, in the end, be thinking?" On the subway, they're sitting side-by-side, a boy and girl, but almost indistinguishable, brother-sister, eroto-siblings, androgyne. They are wearing the standard uniform: white briefs and short white tunic leaving hormone-softened limbs and rounded bellies bare, rubber flip-flops on pale bare feet with silver-painted toes, bleached hair and bleached skin. They sit close together, arms and thighs touching, as if afraid, but few would dare touch them, sacred animals, tagged as they are, property of one of the larger and notoriously well-protected corporation "farms." Even at this lawless hour of the night, two a.m., they are relatively safe from freelance poachers and cannibal outriders. No—it's not fear, but a symbiotic neo-herd instinct induced by a potent mind-control mix of psychotropic drugs, hypnotic de- and re-conditioning, and perpetual low-level sexual arousal which binds them in a shared sense of sociopolitical fatality and the glazed sexualized anticipation of a euthanized necrorgasm, i.e. Heaven. Poachers exist, of course, willing to nab a pair as succulent as this, for resale to other farms or private collectors, but most would prefer to cull cattle from herds easier to raid. And as far as these docile creatures are concerned, it's a matter of the greatest indifference who draws the metaphorical blade across their soft, buttery, and unresisting throats. Slaughter is anonymous. *"It is by magic that the abominable institutions which enclose us: country, family, society, mind, concept, perception, sensation, affect, heart, soul, science, law, justice, right, religion, notions, verb, language, don't correspond to anything real."* *--Antonin Artaud* They winter indoors, in cramped overheated apartments, where they are brought to this maintenance level of submission, fed intravenously with a steady diet of the aforementioned hormones, aphrodisiacal tenderizers, and hallucinogenic psychosexual pharmaceuticals. They spend the great part of their days in an erotic stupor, fondling, caressing, and kissing each other's pretty bodies with narcissistic self-absorption, dozing off to sleep at regular intervals, forever unable to quite reach the orgasm that seems just a touch away. That's what death is for, darlings, is the message broadcast from their medulla oblongata to them night and day. Each succulent pair is assigned a "handler" who checks on them

four times a day. Like a nurse, this handler tends to their basic
needs—including bathing, depilating, and bleaching their bodies as
needed—and facilitates the process that turns them into pretty and
compliant cattle, including the administration of all drugs and
psychotropic agents, both chemical and corporal. A tall, thin Asian
woman in jeans and lizard-skin cowboy boots enters a shoe-box
apartment on Thompson. It's hot as a greenhouse in here, she thinks,
turning up the heat another ten degrees, and peels off her leather
jacket, revealing small tits in a tank-top, whip-thin muscular arms.
The girl is already on the bed, face down, ass up, idly fingering
herself. The boy, not that you can tell, even naked, much difference
between the sexes at this point, is staring, stoned and unseeing, out
the small barred window. Miko sighs, barks a command, and the boy
shakes himself out of a daydream of erotic collapse. He smiles
vaguely and shuffles sleepily to the bed, climbing up beside the girl,
the two of them now lying obediently, faces down, propped on all-
fours. They know the drill. They shimmy down their transparent g-
string thongs and their pert twin asses, situated side by side, await her
ministrations. Cute. Miko takes the dark bottles and sterilized
hypodermics from her bag and lines the tools of her grimly erotic
trade on the room's one small table. Into the ankle, she injects first
the girl and then the boy. Then it's a pair of long injections into each
smooth buttock. No protest at all from the little lambs. Not a peep.
The boy merely gurgles placidly into his pillow. With practiced
fingers, Miko pokes and prods the pliant white flesh. She tests the
boys muscles, coldly asks him to squeeze her finger as hard as he can.
The boy obliges. His grip feels about as powerful as a six-year-old's.
She grunts her approval. They're coming along right on schedule.
::He's almost as weak as you:: She says, turning towards the girl,
who's lightly snoring, an occasional muscle-twitch or finger-flex
indicating that she's already lost in the midst of an erotic dream.
Come autumn, they'll be ready, even now they are free to pass
through the city at will, if you can call their pointless meanderings the
result of anything like "will," riding subways, wandering through
museums, concerts, bars, restaurants, department stores, any public
place at all, where they are completely ignored, or regarded with

expressions variously tolerant, indifferent, or vaguely sympathetic. The way one would look, for instance, at a pair of doomed sheep. In Saks, a little rich girl of eight, dead, sucking on a lollipop stick, turns to stare at an ephemerally androgynous pair as her mother pulls her towards the escalators leading to the fur vault. The half-pint corpse smacks her lips and bares her teeth. Around the city, they've erected what seem to be ordinary radio towers. But these structures are really electronic sentinels broadcasting a reality-inducing frequency that ensures no one leaves. THEY can broadcast any frequency, *any reality*, they want. And so you see the world you see: men and women coming out of the subway station, shoppers looking into shop windows, workers in offices, cops directing traffic, taxis, joggers, dog-walkers, and all of it going on right in the middle of the hellish horrors I've been describing here. Everyone here is in the middle of a pornocalpytic warzone situated in the no-man's land between life and the zombie-dead reanimated from a virulent oblivion—and yet they are sitting leisurely in Starbucks chatting about their kid's soccer camp and sipping iced chocolate frappucinos. You see it only in the hallways of your peripheral vision: a floating black shape forming and re-forming itself like something burning without the flames that's never consumed, an occlusion, a blind-spot that is breathing, a Rorshach blot that is waiting in ambush. A splinter in the eye: that's what vision is. I'm imagining coming home to see how Cherie saran-wrapped your head because you were a fussy little baby. I want to poke a tiny hole in the wrap between your lips so I can hear you struggling to breathe, a soft little whistling sound each time you suck a little air. Hold on a little longer, Suki, and I'll unwrap you. First I want to stand over you, lift my skirt and touch myself until you feel my warm cum spill onto your belly, Cherie will be on her cell, watching. Who do you think she's calling, kitten? *Who do I think she's calling?* Yes, who do you think she's calling?

The Colonel is sitting in a Starbucks somewhere north of 42nd street, plugged in, calmly sipping a coffee, a bitter brew, and listening to the reports of the blitkrieg rolling through SoHo. Canal Street is in

flames, a burning snake of shrieking Chinese and cheap souvenirs all
melting into a tarry slag. Greene, Mott, Thompson…there is
shattered glass, nude corpses, and oily burning piles everywhere. The
dead are battling it out in the corridors of City Hall and the mayor
has been intercepted at a roadblock on a highway entering the city
from the north. The radio stations have all been jammed and seven
military attack helicopters have been downed in the East River. The
Colonel checks his watch: 0724 hours. He takes a sip of coffee.
Everything is going according to plan. But something is still wrong.
Something is always still wrong. The sun, the goddamn burning sun, like a
golden eyeball in the burning asshole of god, how the colonel hates it,
how he glares at it, his mortal enemy, and how he tries to stare it
down and cannot. ::Kill them, kill them all!:: he orders blindly,
slamming both his fists on the table, and he hears his order carried
out immediately, somewhere, a sickly chattering of machine gun fire,
like cynical laughter. But it's not enough: ITS NOT ENOUGH!
::If only I can express the full extent of my rage:: he suddenly hollers,
bolting to his feet and turning over tables in a fit of maddened
frustration as he dashes to and fro, terrifying the other Starbucks
patrons ::if only I could say the word sufficient to explode the sun
this whole rotten world would be destroyed in an instant and for all
infinity! You see:: he says, coming to a stand-still by the rack of
bagged coffee beans and lit quasi-mystically by the track lighting from
above, his voice unanswerable in the sudden deathly silence of the
Starbucks ::I *AM* THE SUN!:: Imagine that, he muses, taking his
seat again in the uneasy hush, the Sun sitting in a Starbucks on the
corner of 8th and 49th on a cool March morning. What a world of
miracles we live in! Oh, and by the way, could someone get me
another cup of coffee? This one seems to have gone…tepid. Outside
the window, a shot-up patrol car slinks passed like some kind of
vicious, ragged, and partially crippled weasel after a fierce fight, but
the uniformed cops inside are cool as Roman numerals: they're dead,
of course. The pornocalypse is already here, all around us, and yet
"they" don't see it. I watch them pass by on the street, sitting in
cafes, getting out of cabs, "normal" people, so called, with the grey
dead bundled like bags on their backs, sucking away their life-force. I

see the zombies stalking them from doorways, following in the anonymous crowd. I see the holes and wounds and voids in their unsuspecting bodies, the so-called living, the exposed viscera, from which something has been greedily ripped away and from which they bleed, constantly, a trail of energy, phosphorescent, like a sexual pheromone to attract the dead. I see the exposed places where they've always *felt* something was missing. That led them to the error of love, of communication, of union. And I see the blood on their faces, smeared all around their mouths, the shreds of flesh and tissue between their teeth when they smile their red and starving smiles—that most specifically "human" expression—traces left from when they last fed on those they love: BECAUSE THEY ARE DEAD TOO. Didn't Jesus say something like this? Life, someone else said (not Jesus), is a gross eating game. Eat and be eaten. Welcome to the cannibal orgy. Garbage trucks thunder up the street, rattling the windows along the avenue, and I see the nude fly-spotted bodies piled inside: thighs, faces, buttocks, hair, feet, breasts smeared with gore and feces—a compressed mass of humanity, a pile of pale meat, hauled off to the landfills. Street cleaning trucks ride close to the curb, brushes and spraying water, washing away the viscera and teeth and gore left behind by last night's party. It's a new morning. Life goes on. Because the dead, my friends, the dead are hungry and THEY must be fed. It's night, suddenly. Just like that, don't try to make sense of the hours, or the lack of them. In a Starbucks again, this one on 3rd and 28th, he's sitting and sipping an identical coffee, plugged in, staring out the window at the smoke rising from the ghostly ruins. He's not the Sun, this time, he's the Anti-Colonel, he's the Moon, not God's enflamed anus, but the cold stone tit that's poisoned us since birth and then hardened forever. He sits there hunched in his black coat, scowling, cheeks shadowed, bald spot, his toenails painted bright red inside his ratty, stinking sneakers.

The whore dancing in the midst of pornocalypse: he invites the universe to fuck him up the ass. The cold stream of infinite stars, a Milky Way, impregnating him with a radioactive futility. This is not, as one might like to think, an affirmation. This is not love. This is whoredom: and this is all there is. $$$, or its equivalent. Smiling lewdly, he stands against the No Parking sign and hikes his skirt up to show his fishnet thigh. He is a fisher of men. It's the morning after, everything sour. ::This bread:: the wizened crone behind the counter assures me, ::was made from the body of a woman. Cost ya dear, dearie:: She cackles: a transceiver planted here by some agency or other. Black market: this sector of the city has been cordoned off, under siege, no supplies coming through. Mass starvation. Men, women, children wasting rapidly as if a fire rages inside them. And it does, it does! Fighting over corpses is the norm. A seven-year-old boy looks like an eighty-year-old woman. No food anywhere. We *are* the food. You have to pay the price no matter what the price.

::She had dark eyes:: the crone cackles, driving up the price, ::shaped like almonds and black bouncing ringlets. Looked a little like a flesh-and-blood Betty Boop:: She squints at me sideways. ::Now I think of it, looked a bit like you, if you were a girl:: She cackles hysterically, like normal laughter taped and replayed backwards. She crumbles a bit of the loaf between her decaying fingertips ::Here, dearie, I'll give you a little taste of what you're buying, sample of heaven, pinch o'cunt...:: Three weeks later, I'm hooked, converted, kneeling at the splintered altar of a bombed-out church, opening my mouth and taking communion from a steroid-pumped ex-fighter in bimbo drag. Behind the altar, in the vandalized sanctum sanctorum, the marble tomb is smashed to smithereens, and a wild hopscotch of dried-up bloody footprints lies in the dust as if whoever belonged to them had been stabbed to death by a mob. *::I AM WHAT I AM::* –*God* Upstairs, in the sweltering attic bedroom, he's lying on his back, panting, his belly swollen with a seasoned fruit-and-bread stuffing, looking as if he were eight month's pregnant, stitched up his bulging center with a thick, flame-resistant black cord. His cock, tied off around the balls, is deep purple, engorged. The sheen on his pale flesh appears at first sight to be merely sweat, but upon closer inspection one sees that a thin coating of spiced cooking oils have been worked into every centimeter of his meat from his scalp to

between his toes. ::Are you still with me honey?:: his wife asks. She's
naked, of course; they've been that way for weeks, the entire family,
ever since their house was commandeered by a militaristic sect of
cannibals. It's unclear if she'll be eaten, too, or eventually adopted
into the sect as a sex-slave and meat breeder, but its understood that
in any event she'll be the last to be eaten. For the time being, her job
is to minister to her family until they're devoured, one by one. ::I'm
sorry I took so long, but I had to tend to the boys:: She describes the
scene downstairs: how she found the younger boy screwing the older
one up the ass in the shower. They've apparently all been given drugs
to increase their libido and put them in a suggestive erotic haze that
helps them accept their current wildly unconventional situation, not
to mention their impending slaughter. It seems that the younger boy,
Joey, barely thirteen, is reacting to the drugs like a jackrabbit in heat,
mounting Charlie at every unguarded opportunity until the latter's
asshole is gaping and bleeding raw. ::Mom:: Charlie whines, his own
hard-on dripping precum on the floor between his bare feet, ::*he won't
stop!*:: Mom, hoping to resolve the bickering, if only temporarily, licks
and jerks each boy off in turn, and then gives her older son a break
by allowing Joey to fuck her in the cunt from which he was shat into
this world. She could only hope that she wasn't too late to minister to
her husband in the attic before he expired of heart failure—or was
carried downstairs and out back to the open pit bar-b-cue. But there
he is, trussed and suffocating. Her husband, gasping for breath, gapes
dumbly at her. ::I'm sorry I had them put you up here:: she explains.
She grabs hold of his oiled genitals by way of consolation, plucked
hairless like the rest of him, and begins to stroke. Though orgasm, at
this point, is well beyond him. ::But I didn't want the boys to see
what they'd done to you. I don't want them to be scared any sooner
than they have to be:: She squeezes her tit and leans forward. ::Do
you want to suck on my nipple?:: At the extreme heights of sexual
excitation, the traveler slips across a border into a zone more real
than the one we ordinarily inhabit. In this zone of eternal warfare,
pestilential fluids, atrocity and throbbing meat, there are no laws we
won't break, no crimes we wont commit, and no tortures to which
we wont submit to approach a suicidal ecstasy. Our suicidal destiny.

Across an endless plain of sexual crucifixions and orgiastic dismemberments, the traveler catches a glimpse of that immense darkness, that indeterminate form, that lurks like a sentient tumor on a horizon of red clouds and oddly punctuated orgiastic screams: the "human being," unmasked, a stifling pollution. This zone, like an extra-dimensional cube of infinite sides and angles, is not distinct from our reality, but interpenetrates it at infinite points, can even be said to be part of it, so that a simple turn of thought or hormonal spurt is enough to find us rounding a corner unexpectedly into pornocalypse. *GREENSBURG, Pa. (March 21) — A couple and their three teenage children held a woman captive for six months, referring to her as their "slave" as they beat her, forced her to do chores and threatened her life and the lives of her relatives, police said. All five members of the family, ranging in age from 43 to 16, were arrested on charges of kidnapping and making terroristic threats. They denied wrongdoing. The accuser, Emily Nicely, 19, said she went to live with the family voluntarily but alleges that she had been forced to stay with them. "She had injuries on every part of her body," said police Capt. George Seranko. A hospital examination also revealed that she had a concussion. Nicely told police that the Pollards became physically abusive, forced her to work and never let her leave the house alone. "She's a liar," Cynthia Pollard told reporters. On numerous occasions, the Pollards punched the victim, kicked her and struck her with objects such as broom handles, a metal pipe, belts and boards, police said in an affidavit. "They told her that if she told anyone or tried to leave, they would put wire around her neck and strangle her," police said. Nicely said she was also punished by having to stand with weights, with her hands on her head or in a corner for hours, police said. Newspaper customer Nelson Williams, 66, and his caretaker called police after seeing Nicely's bruises. "Her face, it looked like a baseball bat hit her," Williams said. "She was bad. Boy, she was bruised."* Oh come on now, stop pretending, admit it, isn't this something you've thought about yourself from time to time? Having a slave to do your bidding? Isn't that what we all want, after all? Isn't that what we need to survive? Someone to feed off of? Stop lying, just this once, just this moment, please stop telling stories, we're all in it together, you know. Think of how you've treated other people, that trail of sucked-empty, discarded lovers you left behind. Still can't see it—or won't you see it? Okay, try this: think of how other people have treated *you*,

how they left *you* sucked-empty, how they've discarded *you*. Better?
Eater, eaten, it's all a matter of perspective here in the pornocalypse.
Like the postcard says, Wish you were here!

Picture this: a man working on his 2005 Federal Income Taxes at the
kitchen table. The back door is suddenly knocked flat off its hinges—
a bang, splinters, shattering glass—and black-clad soldiers burst into
the house. He stares, aghast, shocked, immobile, pencil poised over
Schedule C. Tasered, cuffed, he's bound, gagged, and dragged away
to the center of town where a temporary gallows has been
constructed for the March Fair. Huh? Who knew they had one?
Stripped, hands re-tied, he's hoisted by inches until his straining toes
leave the ornamental gravel of a memorial to the town's fallen World
War I veterans, Meachem, Perkins, Billy Todd, etc. What are the
charges? Don't I get to call a lawyer? Aren't I entitled to a trial? ::Oh
David, please be quiet, won't you?.:: This is absurd…isn't it?
Meanwhile a band strikes up a lively march and cheerleaders from the
local high-school lead the crowd in a ribald chant as he slow-strangles
with several other unfortunates ((the lucky few)) chosen by lottery as
this year's sacrifices. Through eyes screwed tight against the
unbearable red pressure building inside his skull, he spies his wife,
Jenny, in the crowd. In halter top and short-shorts, she looks
incredibly young and sexy, the All- American girl, sipping a
strawberry smoothie, blonde hair tied back in a bouncy pony-tail.
That guy they always see on the 9.07 commuter train into the city,
what's his name, Ted?, he has his arm possessively around her bare
midriff. Bastard! He's feeling up her tits right in front of me! *So that's
what this is really all about!* The corn crop, my ass! Too late now to do
anything about it now. Gurgle-gurgle. His tongue swells up to three
times its normal size, protrudes from his mouth, like a fat blue sock.
He bites it nearly in half. Blood mixed with saliva flows down his
chin like a pink goatee. His eyes bulge like two hardboiled eggs.
Pretty comical if it weren't so gruesome. Still comical, though. Kids
laugh. Splash of sperm on his thigh as the fellow strangling next to

him pops off. Christ, this is insane. His brain shuts down like a city in
a blackout, block by block, there go all those memories from the age
of eleven. Scent of urine and buttered popcorn. Fecal matter. He's
jerking around on the end of the rope, toes pointed, feet fluttering
like a doomed ballerina. Dead, minutes later, he ejaculates. A rose is a
slaughterhouse, a cunt is a trap, a pretty face is what they stick on the
front of a skull full of the same old implacable machinery: survive
survive survive. Copy copy copy. Give us your code, your seed.
Everything that hardens your penis is a lie. Billboards on the side of
the turnpike: Live, live, live. That golden woman stretched out above
the smutty traffic like a vision, floating in the smog above the grim-
faced corpses clutching their steering wheels. Live, live, live…selling
suntan lotion…Yahweh Inc. doesn't want you to spill your seed into
your palm, or to deposit it in a mouth or an asshole because that
doesn't lead to survival, no fake girls, that doesn't lead to *more bodies*,
more death, more cruelty, more fuel, more food. For who? What is it
that eats us in the earth? On 52nd, I see a man walking the latest in
designer pets: a girl in a thong bikini, but *altered*, her lightly-furred
legs engineered overly long which in turn raises her hips up high, pert
ass in the air, plumed white tail, feet shortened to a kind of "human
hoof," which is to say, like a horse's hoof, but with toes. Her walker,
tall and leather-clad, shaved head, multiply pierced—obviously a
butch fag—jerks her along by a leash attached to the studded harness
that fits her like a corset with openings for her twin rows of teats,
four on each side. Her small face, made up to look like an Asian tart,
is worried-looking, it's bred to look that way, but otherwise vacant. If
there's a world after pornocalypse, this is a tiny glimpse of it, as
recorded by a camera on the corner of 8th and 52nd, 7.06 a.m.

It's the first day of Spring, but this year it's the dead that come back.
You see them everywhere in the city, soldiers, white and wet as mealy
worms. (Pull up a crocus or turn over a rock and you see the invasion
of sickly, fever-white soldiers there, everywhere, like pus boiling and
roiling in a wound.) It's like a holiday: from the windows of buildings,

gray, like trembling stacks of cigarette ash the banners hang—a putrid
black stain on soiled deathbed linen, the revolutionary flag. And
Governor Death It's Own Self in full necromilitary regalia rides
through the smoky streets in a sleek white convertible hearse flashing
that well-known rictus grin of victory, but he's not one, he's multiple.
::Its difficult to know me:: the agent says to himself, in a genuine, if
short-lived moment of despair ::I'm a limited gang.:: It feels horrible
to feel the way I do, alone, in a black night, hunting for glimpses of
pornocalypse. But someone has to do it. Truth is, I'm addicted.
::Once you catch sight of it, you don't live to see anything else. Once
you get a taste, no other taste will suffice. Heed my warning.:: Only
the dead ride the bus I'm riding tonight, only the dead are given a
ticket. You must be dead to be permitted outside the perimeter. And
it can't happen by accident either: you've got to do it yourself. Self-
cancellation. ::Suicide, senor. Hardest thing a human ever has to do::
the alien says. ::Go against that old survival program. Exist outside
the existence paradigm. Live outside the box before they put you in it
for keeps, heh-heh. Only the dead are free. But now the hard
part…you must commit an act of violence to do it, and this is the
price of the only freedom worthy of the name. Only way a man *can*
be free, to overcome himself, is to kill himself. Too bad there's no
future in it. Har har har. One of life's little ironies, I guess. Here's the
rope, little pilgrim. Over there's the rusty pipe. Whaddaya say? Got
the intestines for it?:: ::Only a few miles of 'em you bug-eyed grey
little shit.:: And yet, dicking around with the bottle of pills, the plastic
bag, the gun. How long have you got before it's too late, before the
window closes, before they take the choice away? Imagine, though,
an army of warrior-suicides. We could turn this whole fucking planet
into a human graveyard by next Friday. One wonders: what would
come next? An empire of flies, perhaps? Rat dynasties? A socialist
paradise of roaches? Why not? Picture the earth, in this scenario, as a
huge bristling planet-sized asshole, mindlessly buzzing. *PHOENIX,
(September 27) — It seemed like a headache, nothing more. But when pain
killers and a trip to the emergency room didn't fix Aaron Evans, the 14-year-old
asked his dad if he was going to die. "No, no," David Evans remembers saying.
"And here I am burying him." What was bothering Aaron was an amoeba, a*

*microscopic organism called Naegleria fowleri that attacks the body through the
nasal cavity, quickly eating its way to the brain. The doctors said he probably
picked it up while swimming in the balmy shallows of Lake Havasu. Health
officials have put their communities on high alert, telling people to stay away from
warm, standing water. "This is definitely something we need to track," said
Michael Beach, a specialist in water-born illnesses for the Centers for Disease
Control and Prevention. "This is a heat-loving amoeba. As water temperatures go
up, it does better. In future decades, as temperatures rise, we'd expect to see more
cases." Naegleria has been found almost everywhere in lakes, hot springs, even
some swimming pools. Beach said people become infected when they wade through
shallow water and stir up the bottom. The amoeba latches onto the person's
olfactory nerve and destroys tissue as it makes its way up to the brain. Once
infected, most people have little chance of survival. "Usually, from initial exposure
it's fatal within two weeks," Beach said. David Evans has tried to learn as much
as possible about amoebas during the past month. But it still doesn't make much
sense. The questions keep swirling around his head. Why now? Have people
always been in danger? Did city officials know about amoebas? Can they do
anything to kill them off? Evans tried to reassure his son, but he had no idea
what was wrong. On Sept. 17, Aaron stopped breathing as David held him in
his arms. "He was brain dead," David said. "My kids won't ever swim on Lake
Havasu again."* Of her bare feet, I'm thinking, what else? Of placing
them side-by-side on a wooden block and hammering a large iron nail
into each delicate white instep, smashing the bones, flattening them.
The rest of the crucifixion takes place later, or in the blank areas
where I'm not imagining. It's her face that I picture next, as it
registers the shock of realization that she'll never walk again, which
comes shortly before the devastating revelation that her situation is
much, much worse than that. Surrender. That moment, even unto
orgasm. They drag his dead body under her smashed and swollen
feet, his jaws prised open, and the blood that snakes its way between
her straining white toes drips onto his teeth. And someone, snapping
pictures of this touching end-of-marriage tableaux, creates the
beginning of a new sacred iconography. Trembling, her own teeth
grinding and chattering, calves cramped in knots of ferocious pain,
she screams her convulsive, long-repressed hatred at the dead man
beneath her in gobs of spit and gore and then she suddenly lets loose,

first because she cant help it, and then *spitefully*, forcing it out, a violent torrent of sour piss directly on his open face because he didn't save her from this fate. She trembles uncontrollably with a shockingly and unexpectedly violent death-chill. ::It should have been you up here, you faggot bastard!:: Ah, the fairer sex, repository of our hopes, safety deposit box of the human dream. ::Open'er up gentlemen:: he says, standing under the half-conscious woman, hanging, limp and broken on the rosy cross. He flicks her rounded belly. ::Let's get all the slop out on the table, shall we?:: And the guy who says this, yeah, this colonel or pirate or serial killer or double-agent or whatever he is, he's the *hero* of the tale. That's where you're at now. Don't like it? Well, it'll get worse yet. Rage, rage, not against the dying of the light, but against the light itself. The light that violates me, like a photon gang rape. The light that sickens me, like a plague of eyes. *If we're seen, we can't be.* Miserable sun. ::First thing we do:: the Secretary of the Exterior says, ::is fuck up the weather: an endless train of hurricanes, typhoons, storm-clouds rumbling across the sky. Make it rain for eighteen, nineteen days in a row. Have the sun stare at the earth goggle-eyed for two months straight. Everything withers. Depression rampant. Suicide rates spike. And, with their defenses down, gentlemen, we're ready for Phase Two.:: The sun is a mass murderer. Schizotextual terrorism. Being what this is the record of, more or less.

Half-digested, the dead return. Oh god, the soggy, sloppy earth is sick, sick, sick! We're walking on the collapsing roof of a massive grave. Teeth, bile, mud, and chunks of rancid meat. Tarry stools, mucous, shreds of blood, pus, knotted hair, and bone shards. And there she is, rising up out of all of this like a vision. Your salvation: light-blue thermal jacket, tight jeans, big sunglasses, and a mane of bleached hair. She comes up out of the hole in the ground thumbing her cell phone and you wonder, Who could she possibly be talking to? You get up from the table, grab your gear, and track her going south on Lafayette. ::Love is the last con:: the alien says, staring out

the window where a good part of Astor Place is gone. Just gone.
Nothing has replaced it. ::Hardwired into your system. It's what
keeps you going. You can't live without. Ergo, the following tale.::
Tied to a chair, a man, naked, his face muted by the nylon stocking
pulled tight over his head. He's gasping, probably his last, breathing
in the scent of her, strongest on the reinforced triangle of material
that once covered her adulterous cunt. Between his legs, a ragged
crater of blood and white strands, yanked out, dead, indicate where
his genitals use to be. What's he trying to say, anyway, this dying,
mutilated man, what does he want to say to this empty, dusty attic
room? Let's listen close to his last, crotch-scented words: ::*I love you,
[insert name here]*:: Can you believe it? In the end, we all want to tell
someone we love them. We think it'll help us survive, even after
we're gone. We think it'll justify us. Redeem us. ::It's all a lie:: the
alien whispers. It's a small yellow room, like the backroom of porn
shop, maybe it is a porn shop. Lingering stench of antiseptic. Semen.
Anal mucosa. You can't get those smells out, can't cover them up, no
matter how many times Pedro mops up. Everyone in the room is
grim-faced. I'm sitting in a straight-backed chair. Wood. One of them
speaks, expressionless as an insect. ::You're a person of interest, Mr.
Satai. And that's not good.:: As if I didn't know. As if I expected any
different. Recycled air. Still that disinfectant smell—it's giving me a
headache. ::We are going to show you things. Unpleasant things. As a
consequence.:: As a consequence of what, he doesn't say. He simply
stops talking, or broadcasting, the words forming themselves in my
brain, no, not *forming* themselves, but simply rising from the bottom,
or the back of it, and it ain't no angel talking, Mr. Blake. ::Consider
that chair your prison, your cross to bear.:: Beneath my hands,
someone slides a keyboard. My fingerpads rest lightly on the hard
little knots of her spine, so delicate, so familiar, so full of alien energy.
::You're in the labyrinth, Mr. Satai. Your objective is to write your
way out. We're terribly sorry.:: He directs his voice somewhere else,
somewhere I cant see. ::Run the film:: The usual stuff. Summary
executions at 5.30 a.m. on Avenue B. Crucified girls, lamp post
lynchings in the park, ritual sacrifice in the skating rink at Rockefeller
Center, by the side of the Central Park reservoir, under the arch at

Washington Square. But it's not a film, not really, it's a metaphor for
what I'm seeing now, a world either I don't want to see or see
nothing but. This double-vision, being in two worlds at once, is
what's driving me to madness. ::You see your job, Mr. Satai, is not to
reproduce reality, but to destroy it. We don't want you to trace the
line; we want you to *mess it up*. We're not interested in appealing to
appreciators of the grand narrative. We don't want to entertain the
sedentary masses. We're not interesting in demonstrating anything to
the devotees of balance and harmony. We're not out to confirm
anyone's best wishes. We want you to inspire…lunatics, degenerates,
criminals. The type of character who'll go out one afternoon apropos
of nothing in particular and shoot up a multiplex. That kind of thing.
That's the ideal.:: So, its two or three days later and you're standing
deep in Thompkins Square Park where she passes every afternoon on
her way to the health club. You take out your periscoping blow-rifle,
it's a metallic wand that looks like a car antennae, provided by a
shaman on Tenth Avenue, and sight down its length to a place at the
base of her pretty skull. You put the weapon to your lips, and, like
giving her a little kiss from long-distance, you blow. Across the street,
she crumples to her knees and swings smoothly forward from the hip
joints, praying to no Mecca, her forehead head hitting the pavement
like a gate slammed shut. Assassinated: a 27-year-old blonde,
employed by the Gap, single, enjoyed Sudoko and the club scene. *"To
offer an alternative to life in all its forms, to constitute a permanent opposition, a
permanent recourse from life: such is the highest mission of the poet on this earth."*
—Michel Houellebecq Across the street, on Astor Place, they are
building the giant glass mausoleum—a necro-porn palace, a twenty-
five floor tower of dead girls, each nude exhibited inside a crystal
casket, displayed for all to see, a tissue dispenser next to each
entombment for the sentimental. Sniff-sniff. ::Oh but she looks so
peaceful.:: Etcetera. I spend hours in the Asian wing alone.
Wandering the stacks. A heart-shaped face, mouth small as a
lipsticked asshole, *and* a lipsticked asshole like a rosebud mouth, ah
the mortuary art, pale feet like a child's hands clasped in prayer…I
grab a tissue, dab the corners of my eyes, I'm not a monster, I
pretend to have feelings. I remember this one: a few months back in

a Starbucks, the one on Park Avenue, I think, in the 30's, sitting at a
table by the window, five-foot-nothing, leopard-print coat, eyes like
shiny black almonds, reading a text book, art history, I'm sure of it. I
notice the little things. That sweet face, those delicate hands, this
long, sleek black hair that fascinates me even now…that irresistible
cant-touch-me air. I finally brought her down with a heart-zapper at a
Staples on Lexington. ::Clean-up in aisle 3.:: She dropped like a 90-lb
sack of unknowingness right in front of the hole-punchers. Yum,
yum, yum. I stroke myself off and catch it in the tissue as best I can.
Back on the street. Lets stop fucking around my friends: it costs you
plenty to get in here. And once you're in, there's not enough leftover
to get back out. I ask no questions, I tell no lies, everything is
everything. Are you ready my friends, are you? Are you ready? Well,
then, get set and go. It's here already. IT'S THE LONG DARK
NIGHT OF THE ASSHOLE!

In a Red Roof motel under the parkway, room 101, last unit on the
row, he has his anti-Gethsemane. TV talking, he depilates his body
and draws self-portraits in mud-colored pencils and waits for the next
wave of nausea to strangle his guts. The toxins scrub him clean and
everything inside him liquefies and sizzles out in a stinking brown
wash of shit and half-dissolved chunks as he crouches, naked,
plucked bald, and shivering, on the cold porcelain hole. Flush. Flush.
Flush. Giving birth? To what…? Monstrosity? There's so much
rotting inside us. Flush. Flush. Flush. Buddha was wrong. Everything
changes, he said. And then set about trying to find the one
unchanging thing: which he called, enlightenment. But the problem
isn't that things change: it's that every goddamn thing around us
changes—but we don't. No, enlightenment isn't unchanging; it's not
a fixed state. That's only a symptom of the old terror, the old need to
hold on to ourselves in a world without definition or destination.
Enlightenment is mobile, unfixed, schizoid, nomadic, undefined—
and, therefore, not at all. You might just as easily call it: *monstrosity*. A
war machine looking for a war. Or spreading the war itself, like a
disease vector. Or, perhaps, its war itself. War—war all the time.

Later, curled on the bed, sleepless, sick, exhausted, the cell phone
clutched in his hand. *Don't call, don't call, don't call*...he calls. We all talk
in the end. Don't forget it. We all break, babble our confession, spill
our guts. The difference between man and god is that...*man talks*. But
even at the eleventh hour there's no mercy, no understanding, no
communication. There's nothing but the stink of other long-gone
bodies on the sheets. Listening to the trumped-up charges, you
realize there's no hope. They've decided to find you guilty: it has
nothing to do with the truth. It's a function of the universe, like the
cold process that makes a star collapse—and other stars unfold into
hard brilliance. ::Nothing personal out here, mate. Just business.::
And then the bullet behind the left ear. Bang. The galaxy must go on,
you know. If you summed up everything Yahweh ever said when
really pushed to the tits, this would be it. Exhausted, you snuff the
cell with your thumb and slide into a dreamless sleep. In the morning,
the door to room 101 opens and you emerge, eviscerated, dry as a
Pharaoh, stripped to essentials. All this sunlight, shit, but it passes
straight through you. You're fire-proof. The man at the desk takes
your key and your hand, resting lightly on the counter, pauses, before
you decide not to bother ripping the heart right out of his chest.
Instead, with a smile like an ancient artifact, you bid him a "good
morning." At a vending machine, you buy a pack of gum to cover the
stench of decay carried on your breath. And you're on your way. ::Put
all your clothes and personal belongings in this cubicle:: the nurse
says, a variation of how this always goes. Everything off and off you
go down that last mile. The colorless corridor. ::Put on this gown.::
Paper, always disposable. Shuffling off with the rest, processed,
tagged, numbered, you lie there and wait for them to do what they
will do. Another measurement, another injection, and another round
of the same questions. ::Have you eaten anything this morning?:: ::Do
you have anything implanted in your body?:: You lie on a table
surrounded by indecipherable instruments. ::Turn over on your left
side:: Someone's hands at your back, undoing the ties of the paper
gown, exposing the dark access points, the forbidden doorways, the
Do-Not-Enters. This is where they'll remove a perfectly healthy
rectum and give it to some cancer-ridden billionaire or sow alien

spore-seeds in the shadow of your prostate to *reverse germinate.*
When you wake up, you'll be different, but you won't know exactly
how. When you wake up something will be gone, but you won't
know exactly what. The anesthesiologist reappears, but stripped of
her jewelry, nail polish, hair, makeup, nose and mouth, she doesn't
look the same, doesn't look human, and she's not disguising it
anymore. No one is. She looks something like an insectoid biped, but
hopelessly blurred, somehow, hard to see in detail, as if mummified
in cellophane. Her eyes, though, are familiar, *but only because they don't
meet yours.* Everyone keeps up a normal banter, talking about the
weather, the weekend, workmates, lovers, friends…but it's all a secret
symbolic code, like a spoken version of hieroglyphs, to convey
something incomprehensible, something inhuman. The
anesthesiologist holds up a hypodermic the size of a small salami.
::This will make you sleep:: ::Ah but when have I ever been awake?::
::Har-har-har,:: go the doctor and nurse, but I haven't said anything
out loud. Have I? She reaches for the IV tube feeding me/sucking
me empty. Monitors blink and beep, the familiar old tune, the
"doctor" snaps on a pair of latex gloves, the bald technician licks his
cracked lips. ::It's showtime!:: I shift my hips a little and stare at a
silver cabinet handle. My vision shakes a little. I think, Is that it
already? I ask myself, Do I feel anything? Then, there's nothing.

"I've seen the future, brother. It is murder." –Leonard Cohen When I wake
up, here I am. Why, where else would I be? Rain, more rain, rain,
rain, and then more rain every goddammed day from now to the
vanishing point. What's that on the horizon—something black and
ungainly, like an electric chair, but moving, moving awkwardly and
inexorably…moving towards…us.

They're after me now, the black dogs and the hypocritical assassins,
the double agents, the cops, the ex-wives, the tax collectors, the body
snatchers, the identity thieves, and all the other Xs and each and
every all of them carrying ominously slim steel briefcases full of

toxins, invisible agendas, extermination orders, and nuclear bomb
sequences. But I'm giddy now, giddy with the thrill of the chase, even
if it's me that's being chased, no, not "even," but *because* it's me,
especially because it's me that's being chased. I lead them into blind alleys,
dead-ends, into the zombie wastelands, the deadlands, into the stark
shocking glare of pornocalypse. I lead them in circles. I lead them.
Nowhere. They want me. Who knows why? I've got the "x" on my
forehead, had it marking me since birth. ::My god, my god, why did it
have to be his face!:: You see, I carry within me…monstrosity. She's
standing at the snack counter of a Borders Bookstore in Central
Jersey. Tight faded jeans, belly-baring sweater under a short blue
hoodie, brown hair tied back in a saucy ponytail, she's chewing gum
and ordering a chilled drink with a foamy top. Wearing some kind of
nondescript flat-soled clogs, which I can only describe further as the
wrong kind of shoes…she hands over her money, I note, with her left
hand. I imagine her name is…what? Bethany? ::One thousand days::
Dr. Parker says, his rubber finger smeared with my blood and ass-
grease. Like the finger God touched to Adams, ala Michelangelo.
::I've peeked deep inside you, my good fellow. Another one
thousand—and, then, he shrugs ::who knows? It's a crapshoot. Use
them wisely:: The inexplicable has happened, as it always does.
They've let me out of the concentration camp. Thrown the doors
wide open. Is it some kind of trick? You bet your ass it is. Is it a trap?
They're not going to tell you, that's for sure. Instead of dying, I'm
led back to the changing room, where I pull my belongings from the
small metal locker, if anything's missing I'm too grateful to have any
of it back to question. Quickly I dress before they can claim to
bogusly discover "There's been some kind of mistake." Is that the
trick, the old practical joke? Such pratfalls. What hijinks! But then it
occurs to me: there are no mistakes, only misdirections, sleights of
hand. There is no magic, only illusions. I pretend not to notice it:
They're watching me. Cameras in the walls, cameras in the skies,
cameras inside me. Sobbing with relief, I make a hurried cell phone
call to say goodbye to all I love before the rest of the anesthesia is
eaten up by my reawakening insanity. I speak in breathless gasps,
::You don't love me you've never loved me, I wish you'd really loved

me…:: Etc, etc, etc. All the usual, from the beginning of recorded time. The usual answer: the silence of the cold and starry waste. Then I'm out in the parking lot where the sun squints at me in disgusted disbelief as if to say ::You! How the fuck were *you* ever again permitted to see the light of day?:: ::You know:: I think out loud, remembering how it's supposed to rain all the time from now until the end of time ::It's true. The weather man is *always* wrong.:: *"What's losing a face,"* Gary Indiana asks, *"when you've always had two?"* And then, for some reason, we're at the ocean again. It ends where it begins. Piles of nude bodies lying by the sea-fringe. So many dead now that they can't be processed fast enough. Yellow caterpillars parked beside excavated pits into which the entire town of Roselle Park, New Jersey is being shoveled under. The stink blows out to sea. A large seagull stands on a log with a chunk of dark fibrous meat in its beak. A kidney, perhaps? And then it occurs to me what I'm doing here. I'm here to watch the horizon. Why do we always look for hope from the sea? Hope: that was a cancer we succumbed to long ago. A terminal malignancy. Monstrosity. What sickens us most is now the most vital thing about us. What's killing us is all that's keeping us alive. There's nothing marching towards us over that barren salt plain. No gaunt horseman in black with hidden face. Savior-gunslinger. What stretches before us forever is empty of possibilities. What lives in its toxic depths is transparent and shapeless, ectoplasmic, like the ghosts of electrified jellyfish. There is, finally, nothing but surface. In her dead mouth, someone shoves a red apple. A well-manicured hand pats her cold and oiled ass. ::You're all dressed for the party now, sweetheart.:: And what of my face, which looks like a high-security zone impacted by something dark—a truck paced with explosives—originating from the other side of infinity? What you see is not a recognizable expression, although one is accustomed to interpreting it as such. After a while, though, it all becomes clear: this is not a face—it's the site of a crash-landing.

All around me the same thing: one ambulatory barren field after another, shattered by something awful that's struck from deep within,

from limitless inner space. The aliens have landed. But not from
"out there." Do you understand? UFOs=Monstrosity. Their great
flying discs have been drifting over our brains for years, casting their
shadows. They don't land so much as emerge. Asian again, long-dark
hair, tan slacks, black sweater, shoes indeterminate. She's sitting
about midway in a bus en-route to the city. Late 20s, though possibly
anywhere up to mid-30s, can't always tell with Asians, pale, flawless
skin and sharply-defined features: cheekbones, eyebrows, the eyes
themselves. A closed, enigmatic, cold face…until a man at the next
bus stops in the aisle to ask her a question about the schedule and her
expression unfolds with polite subservience. (That's my signal.) I take
a strategic position catty-corner, behind her, to the right. In the blind-
spot. Twenty minutes into the trip, the other ten or twelve passengers
dozing or hypnotized by the monotony of the tire-hum, I put her
down. Squeezing my left eye shut, I fire the neural dart. It strikes her
just under the left jaw, below the delicate shell-like ear. The potency
is perfect, although I'd have preferred to see her squirm a little in her
seat (Note: talk to Talbot, perhaps reduce the dosages?). Her eyes
snap open, stare sightlessly at the bottom of the luggage rack above
her head, the lids rapidly fluttering, 15 or 16 times, before snapping
shut. Her head lolls to the side, mouth open, a thin lavender drool
creeping from the corner, but her bladder doesn't release until the
steep downhill approach to the tunnel, and even then, only in
occasional brief squirts. Control, even in death. Dead? She could be
dreaming…of pornacalypse. Later that night, while masturbating, an
email with the vital stats arrives: Amy Kao, 32, freelance tech
support, unmarried, 1 child (being raised by her parents in Taiwan),
bisexual, 106 pounds.

The Parable of the Cellophane Jesus: Yes, it's time for that, don't
you think so? After all the grim and horror? Time for a little divine
intervention, some help from above, a slice of that old time religion?
I'd say we've all been through enough hell. A little salvation is in
order. He's back—just like he said he'd be. He wasn't pulling our leg.
He's wasn't talking out of his asshole. He's back, better than ever,

well, maybe not better than ever, but he's back, and that's got to be
good for something after all we've put him through, he's back, as
promised, and he's got a few things to say. Actually, he's left me to
do the telling, John the Baptist with his head crudely stitched back
on, (fuck you, Salome), still yakking. Jesus, this time he's short on the
lingual, this time he's keeping it mum, playing it close to the vest; this
time he's done preaching to the choir, trying to wise up the marks,
talking to the fucking wall. Jesus doesn't give a good God damn
whether you get it or not. Jesus is sick to death of all you hypocrites
and fakers. Jesus is not the savior; Jesus did not come to redeem the
world. The world is how it's always been and how it'll always be. Get
used to it. And Jesus, he's no better than any of us. *That* is the
message you, jackasses. You missed it last time. Let me make it
plainer this time because there are a lot of thick morons among us:
Jesus is worse than us! Yes, worse. That is the true meaning of Jesus: to
reveal to us how much worse we are than we think, to disclose the
real nature of the human being. Jesus does not assume the sins of the
world: he *is* the sins of the world. He exposes that he, even He, as a
so-called pure and innocent human being, especially in his guise of
innocence, a Son of God, a Prince of Peace, is nevertheless guilty of
everything. Yes, everything! Jesus is Adam illuminated, psychoanalyzed,
and enlightened. He's Adam without the projection, the transference,
the femme-fatale, the "devil-made-me-do-it." He's Adam no longer
playing the victim and owning up to his own shit. Jesus illustrates the
principle that as human beings we are not merely responsible for all
human sins or have the potential for all human sins, or that we can
forgive all human sins…but that we are actually guilty of each and
every sin ourselves, every horror of mortal flesh, every abomination,
that we are guilty of life itself. That's right, folks. Open up today's
paper. Who caused all those African villagers to starve, who raped
and murdered that little girl in Tuscaloosa, who destroyed the ozone
and laid the great green rainforests to waste? Who are the Chosen
People? Where are your fingers pointing? Who's your daddy? The
more one can admit the worst in oneself the more one is Jesus. This
is the meaning of the spiritual discipline: "the imitation of Christ."
Jesus is a revelation of human nature and what he reveals shatters the

"human" altogether, the myth of the human, the lie of the human, it is a crucifixion, and what is risen up and delivered from death is not the redeemed man, not the man reborn, the man free of "sin," but the man steeped in sin, another being on another plane altogether: the *Afterhuman.* Jesus is each of us, literally! Come on, tell me you didn't suspect this all along. Tell me you didn't see this coming. You, who are always going on and on about your trials and tribulations, the cross you have to bear. You, who feel so persecuted, so misunderstood, tell me you didn't expect to be crucified. Jesus is reviled because he is made of cellophane—because he makes everything inside him visible, all-too-visible—and you can see the unbearable sight of his machinations among the tubes and piping, that ole gross eating game of life. No wonder his priests molested all those choir boys! You shield your eyes, you're your heads away, and shout to Pilate, "Crucify him, Crucify him!" Jesus shows us what we don't want to see: what's inside each and every rotten one of us. Jesus pulls up the rug and the floorboards. He shoves our heads in the toilet. Jesus is crucified precisely because we don't want to see that we are Jesus, too. Being Jesus is no barefoot walk in the park, it's no unending calendar of sunny days. Being Jesus is hard work, it's hell. To be God is to be a virus, to be uncontrollable, to be limitless, to *not know* oneself. How can one know oneself if one is everything? The horror of God, (even to God Itself), is that God is without boundaries, God is not confined or defined, God is everywhere and everyone and therefore God cannot exist! Jesus didn't come to die for the sins of the world, doesn't sit at the right hand of the father, or give a shit about the Good Samaritan. Plain and simple, Jesus shows us all the sins beneath his cellophane flesh. He exposes himself, just like those guys in the park; he shows us what we don't want to see. He shows us that God's sins are our sins, and they are no sins at all, but life itself, to live is to sin, my friends, and this revelation is intolerable to human beings, the realization that we are to blame, and so we must crucify Jesus, this Jesus, that Jesus, whatever Jesus we can find.

   Jesus Christ, Pornographer.
   Jesus Christ, Communist.

Jesus Christ, Assassin.
Jesus Christ, Faggot.
Jesus Christ, Serial Killer.
Jesus Christ, Jew, Arab, Communist, Atheist.
Jesus Christ, F.B.I. Most Wanted
Jesus Christ, Nigger.
Jesus Christ, Oil Billionaire.
Jesus Christ, Crack Addict, Homeless Bum, Lunatic
Jesus Christ, Fuhrer.
Jesus Christ, Necrophiliac.
Jesus Christ, Pederast.

Are you willing to worship him now? Or do you deny him, once, twice, even thrice? You've got to choose. The cock is crowing. It's almost dawn. And they've just tasered Jesus outside a 7-11 in Sunnydale and led him off in handcuffs. Some guy got it all on videotape and sold it to Channel 6. Move over O.J. Get ready for the Trial of the Millennia. Johnnie Cochrane is coming back from the dead. Clarence Darrow, too. Court TV and CNN, baby, this is the big one. Do we acquit? Do we dare?

We must crucify all the cellophane saviors, all the artists and mystics, all the prophets and comedians and wiseacres, all the spree killers and dictators who take it upon themselves to reveal what's inside each and every one of us: because to see ourselves truly, to see the god inside each of ourselves, the pettiness, the jealousy, the rage, the betrayal, the bottomless selfishness, the perverse and polyform lusts and so-called perversions, the absolute void of love, that is the root of all so-called Evil, "the horror, the horror," to truly admit all of this is a revelation that if perceived directly must shatter us— annihilate who we think we are—utterly, thank God. The slow striptease that removes the defenses, the rationalizations, the intellectualizations, the fantasies of what it is to be a human being…to hang there in our hideous nakedness, all sucking tubes and sticky tendrils, *that* and *that only* is the true passion of the Cellophane Jesus. His death on the cross is the enactment of the death of the human that we cannot bear, that we must deflect onto this paragon of honor, this one truly honest being who stands (hangs, burns at the stake, etc.) accused of being a madman, a fool, a thief, a liar, a killer, a coward, a pervert, a selfish, cruel, and smugly self-righteous bastard—everything and anything that we don't want to admit to being ourselves—and doesn't deny it, but admits it, proclaims it, even boasts it from the highest cross he's nailed to, "that's me, that's me," and "Father, why hast Thou forsaken me," because, after all, **I AM WHAT I AM**, which is to say, God, which is to say: *Afterhuman*.

…and, yet, though she herself murdered him in concert with her lover Set, Isis wept for her lost Osiris. She reads, on rainy days, the results of the autopsy. Right eye: the strangled corpses of nine beautiful brunettes of identical size and appearance, all in red evening wear, all with long hair tied in a top-knot at the center of a circle from whose empty hub their pale elegant bodies extend as if spokes on the wheel of a horrible chariot thundering to nowhere, ie: a ritual imagined by a Hollywood mogul. Left eye: a broken pane of glass. The forehead: the concrete divider on a four-lane state superhighway at 2.38am. Ears: (non-existent, like resting mini-cymbals, perhaps a Gypsy's?) Pelvis: a Rorschach blot or even an ancient tribal mask without feathers found in a limestone canyon during an excavation for an execute airport. Right hand: a death threat, anonymous. Genitals: one of those deep-sea creatures that explode on contact with our atmosphere. Teeth: not dice or sugar cubes, but something you don't expect. (The asshole, parenthetically speaking, and not mentioned here, is reminiscent of an eye socket from which the eye has been gouged out, or a mouth without either lips or teeth, ceaselessly and catatonically *sucking*, or, which is the same thing, saying one word, repeatedly. But what it is remains, as of this writing…undetermined). Feet: a lone person clapping in an empty auditorium (see ears, above). The heart?: well, it would too be easy to call this some kind of four-valved warm water mollusk cruelly and fatally exposed, stripped of it's protective shell so instead we'll say "picture a napkin with a cigarette hole burned through…" Enough said? Tongue: something wet, unmentionable, even embarrassing, like a rare species of South American rainforest slug. Ribcage: in the old

Museum of Torture, they used to confine heretics to life sentences in one of these. Left hand: a door, locked.

Pick her out at random. You're sitting at a Starbucks on Astor Place, 6.30am, a grey chill Friday morning. You take your coffee to a table near the windows with a clear view of the subway entrance. They come up out of the ground, vomited up in clumps, the train from nowhere having just pulled in. Here comes another.

Answer: never.

The Academy Awards were given out last night. I'm trying to avoid all news of them. In each category, the winner was a zombie. The presenters, nervous, fumbling with the awards, were raped and torn apart at the various after-parties. You have to figure they knew what was coming. Security omnipresent, but, as usual, protecting who from who, keeping what out, or what in? And still. Charlize Theron disemboweled during the Best Picture presentation. Britney Murphy (or was it Reece Witherspoon, or perhaps Alicia Silverstone) comically decapitated to introduce the Tropical Island number leading into the Lifetime Achievement Award. Well, like I said, I've been trying to avoid the whole extravaganza.

I don't want to be reminded. I don't want anything to do with. If possible, I don't want to see or hear. There wouldn't be anything. Why am I why am I? A sense of her flatness, her superficiality, her one-dimensionality. If I cut her open, for instance, it's as if there couldn't possibly be room for all the interior slop that's necessary to keep us alive. Odd-looking chunks of organic waste on the sidewalks this morning. Purple-red. Human? A foreign couple in the Starbucks. The man tall, bald, overly-animated. The woman blonde, short-haired, in a red-hooded thermal jacket. They are surrounded by

luggage. Refugees. Fugitives. On pilgrimage to some non-existent
Eden. They make a great show of themselves, kissing & hugging, etc.
Are they the last of us, then? The new Adam & Eve? If so, she's too
old, her womb an empty grey bag, its too late, there's nothing left, no
tricks, no surprises, no miracles...except?...no except. It's over. A
pretty Asian woman comes in, another alien, another escapee, orders
a coffee at the counter, and our bald Adam sneaks sideways peeks at
her. Even in the middle of a kiss! Are they Spanish? Who? Scarlet Spa
& Salon. Moonrock Diner. Store for Rent. Strada 57 Ristorante
Italiano: what I see outside the window. All of them deserted, marked
over with graffiti and manifestos, testaments and threats. A hairless
animal lopes, part pig, part hynena, with a human face like a puckered
anus. It's 730am. The doctor scratches some hieroglyphics on a
prescription pad. ::These pills, my boy, these pills.:: He takes a phone
call, but one wonders, is he only pretending? ::Will they cure me
doctor?:: ::Cure is the wrong way to think of it. But they will make the
disease more pleasant:: In his lap, I notice only now, his penis, fat and
white and limp, lies exposed. I order a coffee and a cinnamon donut.
Post No Bills. Jalal Gibran. The author of one of the books this
couple in Starbucks have among their luggage. Are they Middle
Eastern? The life of a solitary scholar: that's what I tell myself I'm
living now. As the streets are lost to the dead, filled with the ominous
emptiness of a trap, like a, like a what? A zombie western? Every day
now is the day before the Apocalypse. I can't imagine the
circumstances under which I'll ever have a woman again. A live one,
that is. What's more, what's worst: I don't even want another one.
How much is the latter responsible for the former? I had an orgasm
this weekend, but it felt like I forced it, more or less. The neutralizing
effects, finally, of the chemically treated water they've pumped into
our sector? Do I even care if I become impotent, or will it just make
life simpler? When will they leave, this foreign couple making such a
spectacle of themselves? Are they from Jupiter? From a secret
underground chamber on the moon? Was that the purpose of landing
there back in the sixties—to hide the last living human couple against
this awful day to come? Someone sneezes. Once. Twice. It seems the
signal for something, but nothing happens. Ever since my morning

coffee, I feel vaguely nauseous. Also nervous. About what? ::That's the thing, doctor. I don't know what. It just comes over me. It just— well, it just takes *possession* of me.:: So there it is, out in the open. ::The pills, my boy, the pills.:: Seeing this or that woman: not wanting any of them. Have I said that before? Said what? Is it the plague now? Is that what's going on? Is anything going on? It's in a mall at the end of the world. I see her, clutching books. I run to her...our arms...we kiss and kiss. ::I knew it would be like this. I knew I would see you today.:: ::I knew it too.:: ::I love you. I love you with all my heart.:: Her eyes so calm, so shining, and her smile, mild, like she were watching children, or dominoes fall exactly the way she set them up to fall. ::I love you. I love you with all my heart.:: And then I realize it's like a wedding vow, ::I do.:: ::I do.::, simple repetition, mirror-image, it's a dream, an illusion, it's what we want—to be married to what is missing from ourselves, no, not just that, more accurately, but not quite it: to be married to our missing self. *"The attitude by which we comprehend what love is: consciousness of the division of what previously was one, of what it is to be thus divided, while you yourself are watching yourself." –Jean Genet.* Only if there is another, do I begin to exist. I have worn the same outfit to work—black cords and black wool turtleneck—for how many days in a row now? Does anyone notice? It's possible that no one does. I barely leave my office. It occurs to me that we're all just faking it, pretending to be busy, to be doing something. Doing what? No one knows. It's a company, twenty-five floors, dedicated to producing absolutely nothing. It doesn't matter. If there is another, I cannot exist. My penis, limp inside my shorts. I don't want any woman. How many times do I have to say that before they believe it? Or is it before I believe it? Whos 'they'? Who's 'I'? If I exist, there cannot be any other. :My dear boy, there are no women left. These pills will help you with that. Now please, for the last time, remove your pants. I must examine your anus.:: In the office today: I slept for nearly two hours. A three-minute conversation with my boss this afternoon. I replay it in my mind for the next three hours. I can't remember a single word she said. Did she actually say anything? Did I?

I was going home at seven, (home, did I actually say that, well, let's let it slide) but then I changed my mind on the way to Port Authority and decided to walk all the way downtown. I'll stay overnight, huddled under a desk, at the old writers club. The riots have commenced. The guy at the next desk, another double-agent, another writer, well whatever, he runs through his preparations for leaving: zip this, snap that, pull on his boots, sit down, stand up, walk off, return, sit down, stand up, snap, zip, on and on, until I want to kill him before he can even reach the streets with his keyboard, his arsenal of pens. Mercer Street bookstore: bought nothing. Most of the shelves bare. Looted. What's left charred, urine-stained. All the reports falsified. No one will love me. I will love no one. Now, out the door, no parachute. I woke up on a couch…somewhere…at 3.45 a.m. all places are the same, space is relative, everywhere is everywhere. Hodge-podge, collage. In the men's room, using a paper towel soaked with hand soap to wipe my armpits and ass-crack. Then I walk the fifty blocks or so to the office. Heads on pikes. Bodies in the gutters. Burned-out busses. The elevator up. Shattered glass. Bullet holes in the reception area. Offices empty. No one is there. No one is ever there. Somehow I never realized that before. Ghosts. Figments of my imagination. Others…? Why do I still report to work? It's a chilly morning. Nonetheless, I think I really should be unfailingly cooperative and polite no matter what, super-sociable, it's the best way to safely cross the borders. The vague, supercilious smile. The small-talk. The ha-ha-ho. In the light, the mask. It's your passport anywhere. Are we there yet? Where? *God saved Lot, you'll remember, so Lot afterward could fuck his daughters, but he froze the wife for looking back. On the surface, that doesn't make a lot of sense. But the radical message of that legend is that incest, sodomy, betrayal and all that are not crimes—only turning back is: rigidified memory, attachment to the past."--* Robert Coover I'm guilty, guilty of everything.

::It's just like I told you officer. When I got here the door was wide open and the music was playing. Blasting, really. That overture to *A*

Charlie Brown Christmas. I think you'd call it the overture. The song
they play in between scenes of that dumb cartoon. That bridges the
action. You know. They made a whole album out of it, like it was real
music. No, I don't. It's not anywhere near Christmas, I realize that.
What can I say? I hate that corny bullshit myself. But that was her,
goddammit, as shallow as a saucer of lukewarm milk. But I loved her.
Not in spite of it. Maybe even *because* of it.:: [Wipes away tears.]
:: Right, anyway, I walked in. I called out first, of course, I didn't live
there anymore, you know? It wasn't my place. She had her own life
now. I'd just come to talk. Anyway there was no answer, so I went
inside. There were flies, that's what I noticed first, all these flies,
covering everything, zig-zagging through the air, and it was cold,
frigid, like all the windows were open, which, as you can see, they are,
but even colder than it was outside. I mean, there was wind blowing
through the place that wasn't blowing anywhere else. It was weird.
Anyway, yes, I could tell something was wrong right off. Even before
I saw the first spray of blood.:: [Pauses, briefly, to collect thoughts
and then resumes in a different voice, smaller, higher, weaker, etc.] I
cant explain it, just a sense, some drop in the atmosphere, you know
how it is, no, I've never been at the scene of anything like this, maybe
its something instinctual, atavistic, some sixth sense encoded in our
genes…still you hope, you know, crazy things, impossible things, that
maybe there was a dramatic, but relatively harmless accident while
slicing an onion, or, you know, a cat lost a paw. No, I'm not joking.
But then you see the viscera on the banister and you think, oh no,
that's a vagina, and it's definitely human. Yes, perhaps that's how the
blood got on my hands, when I was walking up the stairs, gripping
that banister, and then, horrified, I unthinkingly wiped my fingers on
my shirt, and maybe, its true, that's how that bit of tissue, lung did
you say it was, eventually got on my chin, because I was screaming,
or trying to stop myself from doing so, holding my head in horror,
instinct again, I guess, biting my fist crammed into my mouth, easy to
explain then the flesh between my teeth, although I admit I kissed
her when I found her sprawled on the floor, that shovel-handle
rammed all the way up her ass, its all I could think to do, to comfort
her, you might even say, it's absurd, I know, how would that comfort

her, right, I mean, I know that now, but in the moment, you're not thinking straight, you're just reacting. I'd never seen so much blood, it was like ten people were killed there, did anyone find her lover, did she have a lover, I don't know, I just assumed, maybe that's the way its supposed to be, I mean all the blood, maybe that's the way it always is, it probably seems a lot more outside the body than it really is, so dramatic, the color, and the taboo of it, you'd know better than I, but it seemed excessive, unreal, almost like some kind of practical joke. I even started laughing, I think, braying you could say, that's the word you used, isn't it, the word the neighbors used, then, okay, repeating over and over, I don't believe this, I don't believe this, I still don't believe it, you know, and once again I started to consider it was all a dream, some kind of fantasy, the desperate things you tell yourself, you don't know, well, maybe you do, you see these things all the time, don't you, I was in shock, I guess, probably I still am, no, of course I'm not a doctor, I just assume, shock, what is it, I'm not sure, I just assume, I can tell you, I don't feel right, numb, unreal, not myself, is that shock, you tell me, or bring me a doctor, yes, I think I need to see a doctor, I don't feel well. No, I don't remember picking up the knife, or cleaver…whatever it was…I don't know why I would have, because it was there, maybe, its as simple as that, it was lying there and it was inconceivable, like an alien artifact, completely incongruous, plus, I was scared, what if the perpetrator, what if he or she was still about, in hiding, and…and…[subject struggles with speech, falls silent for several moments, resuming after encouragement in a hushed but defiant tone] well, I don't know exactly how to put this, but it had been intimate with her, yes, the cleaver or bayonet or whatever it was, it had been inside her, it had known her, touched her, like I would never…it doesn't make any sense, I see that now, its not rational, not logical, in the light of day, you know…it's love, you know…it's…maybe I'm still in a state of shock, did I say that already? It was her face, officer, her beautiful face, seeing it like that, I don't know how long she'd been lying there, how long she's been dead, is that what always happens, how long did you say, four days, five, no I don't remember where I've been the last week, where did they come from anyway, all those flies, it was like

they appeared out of nowhere, I guess they'd laid them, the eggs, I
mean, its nature, it's what happens, the beautiful face of my beloved
was like a broken plate filled with blood and worms. Yes, I brought it
to my lips, as repulsive as it was…the smell alone was intense,
burning, like inhaling sulfur, I choked down my nausea, I was
sobbing uncontrollably, but I drank from it, sir, it was something I
had to do, something I had to prove, to myself…who else?…that kiss,
that was love, officer, that was love in a nutshell, it's not logical, love
doesn't make any sense, I loved her…there's no doubt left in my
mind…I loved her…:: [End tape].

He bursts into the Starbucks on Broadway, a man I've never seen
before, dressed in a white robe and turban, a black leather golf bag
slung across his back. You can just tell he means trouble. ::Why is
there something:: he screams, sliding what looks like an assault rifle
from the bag instead of a nine-iron ::rather than nothing?:: BAM!—
and the shiny dome of a man's head vanishes in a vapor trail of
powdered glass and bone as the front window buckles and collapses
onto the sidewalk severing the ankles of passersby. The overpriced
knickknacks on the shelves tinkle merrily. Screaming. Nat King Cole
crooning on the sound system, oh please, not "What a Wonderful
World," anything but that. BAM! BAM! BAM! The chest of a white-
haired woman looks like the site of a bloody excavation to unearth
Utopia. A business man in white shirt and blue tie, stirring milk into
his coffee, loses shoulder and arm, the plastic swizzle continues a few
revolutions on its own. Chairs dissolve into sawdust and splinters. A
young woman reading a fat Ayn Rand novel with her morning latte is
cut completely in half on page 438. Paper cups, chair stuffing, coffee
beans all go flying as if caught up in a tornado. At the center,
unmoving, or, rather, revolving slowly as if he were the centrifugal
pivot of this impromptu storm, the man in white turban, pumping his
rifle, spewing rounds like fiery pills, good for what ails ya. Puddles of
gore. The rude slap of wet viscera as it hits the wall. From the edge of
a low table some kind of organ hangs, tubes and tissue a-dangle,
stretching slowly towards the floor like a skinned octopus. Behind the

counter one of the baristas is sitting fork-legged, jawless, in a mixture
of French Roast, urine, and plaster, a shattered phone clutched in his
dead brown hand. Another, a woman of, say fifty (she had some kind
of accent when I ordered, was it Hungarian?), looks as if she tried to
stuff herself into the bullet-ridden pastry case, naked as a plucked
turkey, sloppily butchered. Shredded newspaper falling through the
air like confetti. And the Catholic schoolgirls, did I mention them?
Where did they come from, anyway? Cramming for first-period social
studies, I think I heard one say, an entire table of them by the door,
now a mix-and-match jumble of meat chunks and clotted hair among
scraps of green-and-blue plaid. And the man in the white turban at
the center of it all has finally slowed, then stopped turning, and with
him the room, no longer a carousel of chaos and slaughter, has fallen
still. A shard of glass falls from the window. Silence. I take a sip of
my coffee and realize there is almost none left, too much sugar left
unmelted on the bottom. ::Why is there something:: the man in the
white turban asks quietly now, asks sadly, asks no one, not expecting
an answer, not anymore, how could there be one anyway. ::Wouldn't
it be better:: he whispers, ::If there were nothing?:: I shrug and leave.

So I get up to go. I always get up to go. It's time to go. Well, it's
always time to go. Go where? He's an old man in a white straw
cowboy hat and ratty tweed coat. In his right hand, a thick walking
stick carried like a parade baton. His spotted jowls sag. Mouth
hanging open. Emphysema? He doesn't appear to see very well. He
moves as if he were pushing against a strong north wind, pushing
against a thousand years. And, to top it off, he's walking away,
leading an army of nobody, a parade of silence. He's making his exit,
stage right, up an otherwise empty White Street, west, towards the
setting sun. ::Do you know who that is, Mr. Satai?:: I stare at the
surveillance photo the agent has slid on the table between us. ::No::
::You're absolutely certain you've never seen this man before?:: ::I'm
positive. Who is he?:: The agent frowns. ::That's the hero of our
story, Mr. Satai. What do you think of that?:: ::I think we're in a lot of

trouble.:: ::Is that supposed to be funny, Mr. Satai?:: ::I don't know. Is it?::

.....and the fog rolls in, blanketing the great metropolis, dissolving the walls of the prisons and madhouses, all borders erased, allowing dreams to escape in the multiform of monsters. It's all been planned, you see, up to a point. And then things just kind of happen all by themselves: *pornocalypse*. You can sense it in the air: the storm a-building. **YOU'VE BEEN LIED TO. There *is* a God. He knows you. He loves you. He has a plan.** --the sign on the Times Square Church overlooking the blind masses on Broadway. *This* is part of His plan? *This* is a "plan?" ::Hoist'er up boys:: the foreman says, and two thickset guys in blue hard hats and ConEd gear yank the body off its feet. Slender hands claw at the hairy rope around his neck and slippered feet start pedaling. ::Har har har:: the foreman laughs, re-lighting a cigar stub. His crew heave-ho. The slim body shakes all over. At the crotch, the pink leopard-print leotard is bloodied, torn, exposing a blob of half-tumescent flesh. There aren't many women left in this sector. You have to make due. Are those sequins dusting the high cheekbones like glittering freckles? Oh my! ((Later, when the corpse is abandoned, the pigeons will swarm beneath to peck at the blinking glitter scattered among the spilled semen thinking they are crumbs of magical bread, ie. manna from Heaven.)) You see, they say there is a prophet roaming these streets, huddled under stinking blankets, living in doorways, disguised in filth, hunted by no one, but, nonetheless, in danger of casual assassination ((aren't we all?)), but don't believe it. He's out there, dressed in old newspapers, eating out of trash cans, collecting recyclables, but we don't buy it. He's seen visions, celestial architectures, he's heard voices, read testaments in the sky, he's journeyed across the long dark night of the soul, back and forth, several times, and he's got a message he's muttering into his unkempt and food-stained beard…that's what they say, but trust us, if it were true, you wouldn't want to hear it. That door over there, you know, whatever happens, whatever you do, don't open it. Promise?

Despair is a spotted, long-limbed suicide in action, it's suicide by the
half-second, the slaughter of moments. Despair is a leaping on the
neck of life and sucking it until its knees buckle. Despair is a wild
predator with no natural prey. I hate too much to kill myself. I hate
you, all of you, life itself. I hate like a nuclear holocaust. If I kill
myself…indeed, what is the point? If I kill myself, I give you hope. I
consider despair a predatory super-virus, as well as a spotted, long-
limbed suicide in action, a leaping on the neck, and all the rest.
Despair will be the last virus, the one disease we cannot cure. We will
have to live with it, for it, by it. We will have to merge one with it,
seek our joy in it, our reason to be. What doesn't kill me I become.
Surely I mentioned: there is no cure. It is the cure itself. There is no
self-destruct mechanism in pure despair. As long as there is fuel,
there is the fire. As long as there is life, there is my despair. As long as
I have a breath, I'll curse you, poison you, try to murder you. Pure
despair wants to survive at all costs: it wants to survive to eat up
every hope, every smile, every ideal, every everything. How can I kill
you, if I'm dead? Surely I mentioned it? I hate you. You find me:
asphyxiated, poisoned, car-crashed, shot through the upper palate.
Immediately, you use my death as propaganda. You reinterpret my act
of terror. You turn it into cowardice. Into weakness. Into despair. He
was sad, disappointed, insane. He couldn't cope, couldn't love,
couldn't find happiness. Life controls all the media, the capital, the
sex, the women, the prizes, the fame…it pays off all the novelists,
screenwriters, philosophers, poets, and artists. This is war. War of all
against all. Suicide is written into the rules of conventional warfare,
but despair is the recurring malignancy of terrorism. One bad cell
will do you in. I'll move in stealth. I'll refuse to act with honor,
courage, or principles. I'll refuse to die until I'm slaughtered by the
forces of *good, of God.* I'll refuse defeat because I have no objectives. I
am the ultimate enemy: there is nothing I can consider victory. I am
in the horror movie of life simply this: MONSTER.
Monstrosity=what is uncontainable, inassimilable, incoherent,
indestructible. Suicide is part of the social contract, a special
circumstance, let's call it clause 1313, paragraph 13X. Suicide is an
"honorable" discharge, with a wink and a sigh, it's formal surrender

on the aircraft carrier, it's going to the place of execution with a quiet dignity, even in the worst of circumstances. I'll live as long as possible, spitting, biting, kicking…a pure torrent of virulent nonsense pouring from the hole in the center of my face, eyes cold as buttons in a wintry twilight and when I die it will be because you had to murder me. Suicide is a failure to despair: **suicide is a failure to hate enough.** Only when I can concentrate my hate into an area so microcosmically insignificant it is beyond measurement will the resultant repellent force rebound outward in a blast whose shock waves cause eternal disruptive waves throughout the macrocosmos all the way to its never-endingness like a slap on black jelly, a blast whose epicenter will leave a cold crater, an enigmatic absence, the size of the earth in all that space (a black hole?) what we would otherwise mark with the cenotaph: **I**…only then would I consider self-destruction. And not even then—even then suicide would be a failure, a mercy killing, another way to survive. Do you understand? Despair is an unsatisfiable sadism, a torture machine on the roll, a concentration camp, a weapon of war with no objective but more war, a prolongation of hostilities in perpetuity, an absolute wasteland maker. Despair is delicious. It's neither a meal nor a snack. It's an appetite with no food to satisfy it. *"The flat-lined zombie body, disengaged from all intentional vitality, supports a protracted despair no less immaculate than an ECG whine" –Vauung* Look into my eyes: nothing. I shuffle forward in a pantomime of walking. I am a disguise-person. I am zombie. I eat everything: people, buildings, stars, trees. I am a maggot, a cancer, a plague from Saturn. I consume but I produce nothing, not even a fertilizing shit, only an *unfertilizing* toxic shit, an alien shit. There is nothing growing in my wake. There is no stopping me. The bullets hit me like passersby going in the opposite direction on Madison Avenue. Even my hand, dismembered, will continue to blindly crawl. I am focused, monomaniacally, on the vanishing point. What you see reflected in my eyes, literally, is that distant no-place, that nothing I can never reach, that nothing that is here, inside me, wherever I am. *"The more you think about the exact same thing the more the meaning goes away and the emptier and better you feel." –Andy Warhol* I sit on the sidewalk with a girl's head in my hands like a bloody coconut and I'm staring

towards the barren planes of nothing even in the middle of
Metropolis. Zombie doesn't commit suicide. *Zombie is already dead.*
Zombie is walking nothing. I am not a human being: I am a cold grey
slush carried in a bone urn propelled by an unthinking urge to
nothing. Is it accurate to call despair sentience? Despair is unthinking,
prior to thinking, after-thinking. Despair is zombie-nonspeak.
Despair makes no kind of sense, its no-sense, it's nonsense. I eat a
girl and I'm not satisfied. I eat a policeman, same thing. A soccer
team, no difference. I eat everyone on the African subcontinent, it's
as if I hadn't eaten a thing. My belly's empty. I'm still hungry, dammit.
I despair. I can never be satiated. I cannot die. I cannot formulate
what would satisfy me *because nothing can!* Where is the Zombie
Queen—is she the one I'm looking for? Am I looking for the
zombie-fuck, the spewing of eternal corruptions, the ripening of my
own corpse into virulent incoherence like the climax of a billion
symphonies played backward that renders all listeners deaf? And
blind? Am I looking not *only to die but to keep on dying?* I don't commit
suicide because death is not enough. It's not only that I have no hope.
I have no choice. I despair. I am, therefore I despair. I despair like
other men love. If I want to exist, I despair. I despair with my teeth
bared. I despair with a hard-on. I despair like the foreplay of an
orgasm that never comes! *"A call that must be without expectation, without
any possibility of relief or fulfillment, and also which arises spontaneously,
unchosen and inevitable at a threshold of absolute, indefinitely prolonged
abandonment. —Vauung* Where hatred meets despair is at zombie.
Where zombie is there you'll find an intersection with two blank
signs: you are standing on the corner of nowhere and noplace. In
three seconds you will be nothing but a ragged red ribcage and a
blood-slicked femur. Are you not zombie, too? Despair is the dead-
end intersection where zombie waits. Zombie is an eating machine: a
rage without purpose. A bitter wind. Are you not zombie, too?
Zombie is a mastication process: ultimate violence without reflection.
It's an anti-strategy for dissolving everything into chaos. I am
multiplying *unnaturally.* To kill me now, you'd need a flamethrower.
There are too many of me! I am an assemblage of dead parts. Of all
the dead and the dead to come. Are you not zombie, too? My despair

is uncontrollable, like an infectious fog, it spreads over the verdant landscape. My breath is rotten. I am a machine for producing this fog, my jism carries it, the saliva in my rabid bite spreads it. But what animates me? Rage. Hatred. My offspring is misery. Are you not zombie, too? Suicide is a hopeful prophylactic, an attempt to end this misery, to abort the suffering. Suicide is an expression of hope, that I will find relief, that the world can end, that despair can, at last, be snuffed out. Rest in peace. I deliberately practice unsafe sex: I ooze. Despair is a desire that oozes. Look at my clumsy movements, my goose-step, my salute: racism, militarism, capitalism, imperialism, communism, modernism, fanaticism, any-ism that represents the worst possible choice, the "clumsiest" option, that represents the maximum incoherence, that promotes total breakdown, optimum horror, that works as a solvent to melt everything down to dumb inert lump—these are all my anti-strategies, my preferred choices. Zombie is dumb: it is an incoherent crawling goop. Is it dumb to hate—then that's what I do. Is it ineffectual to rage and rape? No doubt. Watch me. I rage and rape unthinkingly like a machine. I don't, strictly speaking, "choose" so much as *tend,* choice is an illusion, I tend toward the most violent, the most obscene, the most stupid. I have a natural affinity for the rank and rotten . Decomposition is *easy,* it's a seduction. I have a natural affinity for a slide into decay. The world is my body is dead is the world that I'd kill. I'm super-superimposed: I'm both zombie and land of the living dead. Open me up: see the dead city, the necropolis of slime. Are you not zombie, too? My rictus grin.

Derangement of the senses, is our only salvation, the only cure for death. What does it mean to say *merely?* What does it mean to say *merely nihilism, merely solipsism?* What I say instead is *precisely.* I say whatever is devalued and dismissed out of hand *precisely* for not participating by the generally established rules of the communal debate there we must find the secret elixir if it should exist at all— among those "dead ends" one might find what is most fiercely viral, what has absolutely no survival value, what begins the terminal countdown to orgasmic self-extinction. ...*or, better yet, a count upward that must be suspended before it comes to any end.* Whatever accepts no counter-argument is what is most apocalyptically feared: gunshot, vomit, blast-off, explosion, masturbation, shit, monologue. But also what offers no resistance: apathy, surrender, diarrhea, alliance, complicity, anal sex, payoffs. *I don't care what you think.* Logic, reason, dialogue are inherently weaker than solipsistic rant—and also impotent in the face of pure nonsense and farce. For the same reason: democracy is weaker than fascism *to reach a goal.* Survival is weaker than destruction. I compromise my revelation when I listen to what you say. I weaken myself by asking for directions. I stand on the balcony, speaking in tongues, gesticulating wildly, foam-flecked lips and dilated eyes fixed on cold nothing. I am pure speed, one-way velocity. The probability that I miss the target increases dramatically the slower I travel. The more I listen to what you say, to what I say, the more chance I have to *survive.* Or I may just as easily be a formless jelly: a goop that can be molded into anything but that eventually dissolves its mold to form a shapeless puddle on the floor. I am a running sore, an *oozing* sore. I listen to everything: I am a tape recorder that plays back everything but that repeats it in a funny voice. I am a closed system. Either speed and fanaticism...or its polar (cold) opposite: the reverse acceleration of decay. Either a steel death mask speeding forward at 800 m.p.h. decapitating anyone standing in the way or a camouflage camaraderie that insinuates itself parasitically into your system may well be as unconscious of itself as it is duplicitous—and, best of all, even *unconsciously duplicitous.* I am ferociously opportunistic: hand out, bent-over, the ultimate company man. I attach myself to anything. I am a free radical whose receptors are an *indrawn suck.* I am a double-agent flip-flop unknown even to myself. I burrow down quietly into the meat of any-body, an anti-body, gnawing away in a cocoon that may just as well be called an encapsulated pustule because it signals the onset of the only thing that can possibly emerge from within such a hothouse sickroom chamber: the rabidity of decay, of shambling monstrosity. I am the symptom of an outbreak of an unnamable disease when it is too late to cure. The possibilities of solipsism as an anti-systematic means of ecstatic personal de-construction need to be encouraged. Autism, catatonia, senility, dementia—these are all other words for simulations of a privatized paradise beyond the out reach of reason, colonialism, oppression. A unicellular revolution: I mutate as does a cancer cell—the metastases begins in singular solipsistic disregard for community. Religious mystics have always practiced and recorded the solipsistic meltdown. One might reasonably suspect that "human" beings in general are always operating by solipsistic programs. They only pretend to abandon solipsism when they come in contact with other "human" beings and find themselves under propaganda pressure to *act* "reasonably" and "responsibly," in other words: to survive and respect the survival rights of the other. Cooperation is mass denial. We *know*, after all, only what we *know*. What consensus reality might we destroy by the encouragement of a voluntary and deliberate descent into solipsism? What systematic crash and short-circuit might an anti-strategically weapon-grade deployment of solipsism cause on every level if it were only acknowledged for what it already is: *the state of things as they actually are?* I dream of a nation of Alzheimer's patients, of everyone forgetting how to use a fork. Everyone, for instance, will have their own private word for "shoelace." Is solipsism "merely" a dead-end? What does it really mean for something to be a "dead-end?" Who marked the roads? And what if one does not heed the sign? What if one goes beyond the "dead end"? Where are we then? What are they hiding? I am a maggot-form at the center of a suppurating Slop-ism. I only half-digest and vomit what I half-ingest and vomit and then I half-ingest it to vomit it again, *ad nauseam*. I keep nothing that doesn't make me incessantly *wriggle*. I am unburdened by any facts. While you assemble your arguments, refute or insult me, defeat me point by exhaustive point, I've already cut out your lower intestines. Your head is still talking but on a pike, your body has already collapsed, an empty shit-sack that the rats are poking their pointy snouts into. You don't hear over your logic-drone, the incoherent buzzing of the flies. I am covered in your blood and shit, dancing like Shiva, all snaky arms and legs, destroying and creating illusions, grime and stars beneath my toenails, emphatically pointing here and there at nothing, a dervish of misdirection, tongue lolling out, adorned with a necklace of skulls: *I am a cross-dressed Kali*. I am a poisonous gas, ejaculated seed—uncontainable. I get all over everything. Solipsism, like glossalalia, is "holy." When what I say doesn't make any sense, when I refuse communication *but won't stop talking*, I approach the "truth" about the incoherence of everything. Does this make communication impossible? Is communication even possible to begin with? Have you ever truly communicated anything to anyone? How do you know? Who cares? Do you think I have any interest in what you say? I make sense only when I vomit. What is it that you could say to me that would really make any difference anyway, that I won't assimilate into a form of what I already knew before you even opened your mouth, your teeth clenched, holding back your own vomit? We are only puking at each other. Look at the mess we've made. Vomit is the incoherence of everything: it is a universe of hard nodules, foul chunks, seedy slime, of the indigestible. I am full of poisons, toxins, lies, half-truths. I want only that which will make me puke better my own puke. I read and listen and watch like an industrial cannibalization project: everything is "merely" raw material for conversion to the energy that is required to fuel my own insatiable maggot-hunger for a private regurgitation. That's it: I eat to have the energy and material to excrete. I am a wasteland producing machine moving across the plains of serious (survival) discourse sowing non-sense: behind me are uninterrupted nothing-fields of solidified puke. Solipsism is like a magick spell: all magick incantations are solipsistic. All texts upon which magick spells are inscribed are wastepaper, useless, spoiled and soiled like used toilet wipes or tissues crusted with dried ejaculate, the moment following orgasm. The written spell, like pornography, is only valid at the one-point: the instant when the incantation reaches its zenith, its orgasm-flash. After that, it's garbage. What you are reading now, for instance, is nothing but a dead cum-stain. All magicians are self-contained systems, closed universes, laws unto themselves, solipsists. The solipsistic text is not lucid any more than the terminal series of images bringing one to climax in an act of sex magick or ordinary orgasm is lucid: these spells are intended only to achieve certain limited *results*, and success

or failure is defined in a fiercely autocratic personal manner without
any consideration for proof by repetition or the outside whatsoever.
If I orgasm, it is a success. If anything at all, it's the unapologetic manner
of solipsistic composition that may be of objective interest to the
outside world, that may "communicate" something to an audience,
but only incidentally (the way a knife is of universal use as a murder
weapon, for instance, but the victim is always personal): I have
ultimately nothing to *communicate* but method, and that only by
accident. *This is the way I stab.* The outside world, the hypothetical
readers of my text, are only innocent bystanders: the "accident" itself
concerns only the actual participant, which is to say, the perpetrator--
and not even any victim. This text is a crime that goes unpunished. I am
my sole audience: I write like I masturbate. I write like I commit
murder. Solipsism is a sentient terminal disease with neither love nor
hate for its host. Solipsism destroys itself as it destroys what it feeds
upon: a parasite without past or future. Solipsism is a parasitical
present that erases itself and leaves no trace. The solipsist is the
ultimate escape-artist. Solipsism is the ultimate escape, a disappearing
act, the chains and padlocks and straitjacket left behind. I write like I
commit suicide—and every text is a suicide note but what I'm
slaughtering is the world. Solipsism is a murder-suicide pact between
me and the world. Solipsism is the autoerotic intimacy of a fatal
single-car accident. Solipsism is whatever I say it is. I am dead to you.
When you read this text you are performing either an autopsy or an
act of necrophilia. You are scanning the front page of a supermarket
tabloid announcing the birth of alien twins destined to become the
saviors of Earth to a raped and martyred Jennifer Anniston shown
naked and dead nailed to a cross in the Nevada desert: there is not
even the pretence of truth to this story. And if I'm wrong and love
can exist between one person and another, love without vampirism,
equations, and the calculation of needs, but true love as we often
imagine it—then life, and all the consequences of our mortality, well
what of it then? It would truly be an agony too horrible to bear. Ha!
There are jokes that only the Gods can laugh at. I hang my head. *"It
is done."* –*Jesus Christ.*

[interruption of tone].

This is only a test. Gasp. Sigh. The old Boo-Hoo. Boo Who? This is only a test. (sound of voice clearing). If this were an actual emergency. If. (sound of laughter) We interrupt this regularly scheduled broadcast. Well, if this were an actual emergency. A test, did we say that? Yeah, this is only a test. It's a test of...what...your patience, your intestinal fortitude, your sanity? It's a test of the Emergency Broadcasting System. That's what it is. If this were an actual emergency, you would have been given instructions of where to turn. He nudges me and points to a table: there's her coat, some petite plaid thing. She's probably claimed the table and gotten up to get her food. Just seeing her coat I feel instantly panicked and nervous. I decide to try to find her before she gets back to the table in order to say just a few words in private. You see now, if this were an actual emergency, you would have been given instructions of where to turn in your own neighborhood. We would be telling you, you see, what to do in an actual emergency. I walk around and around but I can't find her. Finally I start back to the table and I see she's sitting there already. I back up into the hallway and I can barely breathe. I can barely stand. I'm gasping. I'm touching the wall for balance. I tell myself, "Well at least when she sees you like this she'll realize how much you love her. She'll be touched. She can't help but be touched." You would have been given a lot of instructions, a lot of gobbledygook about what to do, where to go, and all that jazz by someone who doesn't know their ass from a hole in the ground. This is what happens in an actual emergency. Because right then the exact opposite thought occurs to me. "No, she won't be touched at all. She'll see you as weak, as exactly the kind of man she didn't want in the first place and rejected." You see, Plato said that we are all looking for the other half of us, that the spell of tenderness, trust, and unselfishness with which we fall under is a miracle; lovers no longer want to be apart, not even for a moment. And in this way all true lovers spend their lives as one, without ever being able to say what they expect from one another; for it's not the dear one's body, or resources, or even their own self-interest that these two lovers seek in each other. But something else…and what it is they cannot say, cannot ever say, and that never-answered-question, that is love. Sorry about that. The fucking aforementioned regularly scheduled programming. Goddammit, it's hard to get it off the air. You have no idea. Listen, like we said, we interrupt our regularly scheduled programming to bring you a test. A test of the Emergency Broadcast System. We're really proud of this test, it's stood us in good stead for a long time, you *really* have no idea. No clue. You see, in an actual emergency. She's sort of slouched in her chair, a wool cap on her head. She looks up and gives a polite little "oh it's nice to see you smile" like you'd smile at a puppy. Her face is beautiful, more beautiful than in real life, like its being shot with a soft-focus camera. I can barely talk. I manage to ask her if I can have a few words with her alone. She doesn't think that's a good idea. Does she think I'm going to hurt her? Is she afraid of me now? I just want to talk to her. I just want three minutes. Cut the fucking tape, Maynard. Jesus H. Stop clowning around. This is an emergency. (clearing of throat) You see, in an actual emergency you would have been told where to turn. Where to turn? (laughter) *Where to turn?* (laughter, two, three, four voices, monkey-house stuff) Oh who am I kidding? Let me be honest for a change. There ain't nowhere to turn. We interrupt this regularly scheduled broadcast to report that massive explosions have rocked the center of our world, our major cities have crumbled to the ground, the sky is on fire, and the water is poisoned. You can kiss your asses goodbye, suckers! People are killing each other indiscriminately in the street. The army is indistinguishable from the citizen. When has it not been? Everything is out of control. You tell me, *when has it not been?* Escape is impossible. *You tell me,* When has it ever been? There is no Law. It was all a sham, all an illusion, all of it. We admit it. **This is an actual emergency.** *When has it not been?* Okay? Happy now? You wanted the truth, you got it. You've been practicing for it all your life. This is it. Stop being such a goddamn victim. Get up off your ass. Figure it out yourself. We've been giving you instructions for years. Have they ever helped? Think about it. Have they? The truth is, it's been an actual emergency all along. We can't tell you where to go or what to do. We don't know ourselves. You're on your own. You always have been. Everything is falling apart. You are the chair which is falling through the floor which is the soil under your feet which is the bedrock of the earth which is swallowed by the sun which is exploding forever and ever into the cold oblivion of empty space. Empty space. Everything is everything. **This is an actual emergency**. It is so, so, so over. You would have been given instructions on where to turn if it weren't. Trust me. You would have been told a lot of lies. You would have been told what to do. *When have you not been?* If there were an actual emergency. You would have been told. In your area. To turn. Where.

[laughter].

[long silence].

[uninterrupted tone].

Don't miss these other
exciting titles from

AFTERHUMAN PRESS
...what's next in books

Hardcore Romeo
Mark Nadja

61 Bang
Mark Nadja

Afterhuman
Michael Cross

The Maniac Manifesto
Nick Caligari

Fake Girls
Matthew Sloan

For more information and free previews of all our books please visit
our website at www.afterhuman-press.com

www.ingramcontent.com/pod-product-compliance
Lightning Source LLC
Chambersburg PA
CBHW020618130626
46552CB00003B/1026